A Fateful Sentence

Lucy Averill

AnniesFiction.com

Books in the Secrets of the Castleton Manor Library series

A Novel Murder
Bitter Words
The Grim Reader
A Deadly Chapter
An Autographed Mystery
Second Edition Death
A Crime Well Versed
A Murder Unscripted
Pride and Publishing
A Literary Offense
Up to Noir Good
For Letter or Worse
On Pens and Needles
Ink or Swim
Tell No Tales
Page Fright
A Fatal Yarn
Read Between the Crimes
From Fable to Grave
A Fateful Sentence
Cloak and Grammar
A Lost Clause
A Thorny Plot
A Scary Tale Wedding

A Fateful Sentence
Copyright © 2019, 2023 Annie's.

All rights reserved. No part of this publication may be reproduced, stored in a retrieval system, or transmitted in any form or by any means—electronic, mechanical, photocopying, recording or otherwise—without the prior written permission of the publisher. The only exception is brief quotations in printed reviews. For information address Annie's, 306 East Parr Road, Berne, Indiana 46711-1138.

The characters and events in this book are fictional, and any resemblance to actual persons or events is coincidental.

Library of Congress-in-Publication Data
A Fateful Sentence / by Lucy Averill
p. cm.
ISBN: 978-1-64025-255-4
I. Title
             2018958568

AnniesFiction.com
(800) 282-6643
Secrets of the Castleton Manor Library™
Series Creator: Shari Lohner
Series Editor: Lorie Jones
Cover Illustrator: Jesse Reisch

10 11 12 13 14 | Printed in China | 9 8

1

Faith Newberry leaned back in her desk chair, stroking the soft fur of the black-and-white tuxedo cat purring softly in her lap, and gave a contented sigh.

It had been a quiet morning in the library, and Faith had taken the opportunity to catch up on e-mails, catalog some new acquisitions, and review the upcoming retreat. As librarian and archivist, Faith was responsible for the thousands of volumes and documents around her. The place wouldn't be quiet for long, though, so she and her cat, Watson, savored the peace while they could.

Castleton Manor, a breathtaking French Renaissance château-style mansion on Cape Cod, Massachusetts, hosted numerous book-related events throughout the year. Guests would soon be arriving for a retreat on memoir writing. Several writing groups from around the country would convene at the manor. The small groups would mainly meet separately for workshops, but there were a few special events planned that would bring all the writers together.

She didn't need to inspect the ornate woodwork or run a white-gloved finger over the elegant mantel to know that not a speck of dust had accumulated anywhere. The housekeeping staff and all the others who kept the manor running were meticulous in their work.

Faith's own job was one most librarians could only dream of. Unlike many public institutions, the library at Castleton Manor did not rely on outside funds to operate. The manor's co-owner, Wolfe Jaxon, was a passionate collector and an enthusiastic reader, and he enjoyed spending some of his considerable wealth filling the shelves. He and his mother, Charlotte, also endowed the public library in the nearby village of Lighthouse Bay.

Her heart grew warm inside her chest. She and Wolfe had recently taken their friendship a step further and had officially started dating. Faith didn't know where this change in their relationship would lead, but she liked the direction it was headed.

Faith gave Watson one more stroke from his head to his stub of a tail, which he'd lost before she rescued him in Boston years ago. "How about a walk, Rumpy?"

Watson jumped down from her lap and stalked to the terrace door. He glared over his shoulder at her, his eyes glittering slits. Obviously, he didn't appreciate her using the nickname.

She followed him out the door, then locked it behind her.

As soon as they stepped outside, Faith breathed in the salty air. The breeze from the shore ruffled her hair as she and Watson made their way along a wide path to a field at the far edge of the property.

Some time ago, Charlotte had requested a tribute to Laura Ingalls Wilder, and Wolfe had been only too happy to indulge his mother. He went above and beyond by hiring an architect to design and oversee the project of adding a log cabin to the manor's meticulously designed grounds. A line of trees obscured this part of the property from the manor, so the incongruous structure would not appear out of place. It certainly would have been odd next to the extravagant gardens, but it was perfectly charming in the grassy area on the other side of them, bordered by trees.

Faith felt a thrill of excitement. She'd loved the Little House on the Prairie series as a child—and she still did. The log cabin was scheduled to be completed today, just in time for the writers retreat. Pamela Browning, one of the group leaders, planned to use the books of Laura Ingalls Wilder as examples in her workshops. Her small group would be meeting at the log cabin throughout the retreat.

When Faith reached the log cabin with Watson at her heels, she saw the architect emerging from the building. Philip Peters was a tall man with a full head of brown hair and pale-gray eyes framed by tortoiseshell glasses that gave him a studious appearance.

Philip smiled warmly. "Have you come for a sneak peek?"

"I've been on pins and needles all morning," Faith admitted. "I can hardly wait to see what you've done in there."

"Come take a look." Philip beckoned her inside with a magnanimous sweep of his arm.

As if he'd been waiting for an invitation, Watson raced inside ahead of her.

As Faith stepped inside the cabin, the unmistakable smell of freshly sawn wood filled her nostrils.

Philip followed them inside but stayed near the door, allowing her to explore the space on her own.

The interior consisted of one large room, and the walls were constructed of logs that shone with a golden patina, which Faith imagined would darken as the years went on. She was reminded of the library in the manor with its rich wood paneling. It was almost as if this cabin were a smaller and simpler version of Castleton Manor. The thought amused her, and she smiled.

Faith was also pleased to see that some of her recommendations, based on her thorough study of the Laura Ingalls Wilder books, had been implemented. A potbellied woodstove took pride of place in one corner of the living area, and a rudimentary kitchen and a large table with six chairs anchored the other end of the room. A wooden ladder gave access to a second-floor loft.

"Is the sleeping area finished?" Faith asked.

"Everything is set to welcome the writers as soon as they arrive," Philip said.

Faith laughed. "No one will actually be staying here during this retreat, but I'd love to see what it looks like."

"Be my guest," Philip said.

Faith climbed the ladder and entered the sleeping loft, where sunlight streamed through small windows set into each end of the room. Tucked up under the eaves of the low-ceilinged space were four comfortable-looking beds, topped with beautiful handmade quilts. Nestled into the gable end of the loft was a small stand. A china washbasin and matching pitcher had been placed on it, complete with a fluffy white towel. The effect was absolutely charming.

She couldn't wait for her aunt to visit the cabin. Eileen Piper was the head librarian of the Candle House Library in downtown Lighthouse Bay and an adamant supporter of children's literature.

After a final admiring glance around, Faith descended the ladder and joined Watson in front of the woodstove.

"What do you think?" Philip asked.

"It's absolutely lovely," she said. "I would have thoroughly enjoyed spending time here as a child. I'm sure all the guests will feel the same way."

"I certainly hope so," Philip said. "And I expect that the future children's events will also be popular."

After its inaugural use by the memoirists, the cabin was one of the ways the Jaxons planned to expand into offering more family-friendly events at the manor.

"I'm meeting my wife, Janine, for lunch," Philip said. "Would you care to walk to the manor with me?"

"Thanks for the offer, but I'd like to stay and explore the cabin," Faith said. "Enjoy your lunch. Brooke Milner, our head chef, has prepared clam chowder and crab cakes with a native field greens salad today. You're in for a treat."

"It sounds like it. I'd better hurry." Philip turned and strode off.

After Philip left, Faith spent a few more moments examining the cabin's details, including a full set of the Little House on the Prairie books and several biographies of the author that Faith had curated. Satisfied that everything was ready for the guests, she exited the cabin.

Watson followed and sat down in a patch of sun on the step.

As Faith closed the cabin door, an odd rumbling sound caught her attention. "What do you suppose that is?" she asked her cat.

Watson groomed his paw, apparently unconcerned.

Faith stared in amazement as a covered wagon came into view. A dapple-gray horse pulled it, and a woman in a poke bonnet and a prairie skirt sat on the driver's seat with the reins in her hands. Within a few feet of the cabin, she pulled back on the reins. The horse and wagon stopped.

Watson pressed against Faith's leg. She was sure he was as surprised by the contraption as she was. The cat had some familiarity with horses, but the covered wagon was a new experience for both of them.

The woman in the bonnet hopped down from the seat and patted the horse's flank before turning to Faith. "Good afternoon. I'm Pamela Browning, one of the facilitators of the retreat." She extended her hand.

Faith smiled as she shook the woman's hand. "I've been looking forward to meeting you. I'm Faith Newberry, the librarian. Welcome to Castleton Manor."

"Thank you," Pamela said, then glanced around at the beautifully tended grounds. "What a lovely spot for the cabin."

"It certainly is." Faith gestured toward the covered wagon. "You seem to have chosen the right transportation to get into the pioneer spirit." Had Pamela driven this vehicle through the streets of Lighthouse Bay?

"I thought it would be the perfect opportunity to take Stormy and the wagon on a jaunt," Pamela said. She adjusted her bonnet and retied the strings. "What's the use of having a covered wagon if you can't share it with anyone else?"

"How far was your trip?" Faith asked.

"I only drove it from the parking lot where the flatbed truck dropped it off. I brought Stormy in his trailer, which I parked with my truck near the stables."

Faith nodded as she studied the conveyance. "Is this the same kind of wagon the Ingalls family would have used?"

"It's a good replica, but it's smaller than the prairie schooners that took most of our settlers, including the Ingalls family, west in the nineteenth century."

"I'm certain everyone will enjoy seeing the wagon," Faith said.

"One thing is for sure," Pamela said. "It will definitely attract attention."

"I'm a big fan of Laura Ingalls Wilder's books," Faith said. "I was excited to hear that you plan to use her work in your curriculum for the retreat."

"Although she wrote more fictionalized accounts, I think the basic principles for writing memoirs still apply," Pamela said. "I'm confident the writers will learn from her. Hopefully, it'll be an unforgettable experience for everyone. Will you be attending the workshops?"

"Unfortunately, no. Although I would be more than happy to assist you if you need anything."

"Now that you mention it, I would love to see the library's collection of Wilder books," Pamela said. "Would it be possible to borrow some of them during my stay?"

"Of course," Faith said. "The Little House on the Prairie series and several biographies are already inside the cabin, but I'll gather some other materials about her."

"That would be wonderful. They'll be very helpful during my workshops." Pamela gestured toward the log cabin. "And I'm sure it'll be inspiring for my students to work inside that adorable building."

"Would you like to peek inside?" Faith asked.

"Oh, can we?" Pamela's eyes sparkled.

Watson stayed outside while Faith ushered Pamela into the cabin and showed her around.

Pamela inspected every inch of the cozy structure, oohing and aahing over the smallest details.

By the time they finished the short tour, Pamela's face was flushed with excitement. "It's even better than I had imagined it would be. Everything is perfect. I can almost hear the wind—and the wolves—howling outside."

"The architect did a wonderful job," Faith agreed as they walked outside.

Pamela went over to her horse and patted him. "I should get Stormy situated at the stables. I'm sure he's ready to have a long drink and a meal."

"I should be heading back too," Faith said. She scanned the area for Watson, but she didn't see him. Not that she was particularly worried. Watson was quite capable of getting back to the manor or to Faith's cottage on the grounds.

"How about a ride in the wagon as far as the stables?" Pamela offered as she climbed into the seat. "I do love to drive this thing, and it's more fun with a passenger."

"That sounds great." Faith's heart leaped in her chest. Many times she had imagined herself riding in the covered wagon with young Laura and the rest of the Ingalls family. She clambered up onto the seat next to Pamela.

Watson popped out from under the white canvas and jumped nimbly to the ground as the conveyance started to move. The cat took off in front of them, leading the way from a safe distance. He remained several yards in front of the horse's hooves all the way to the stables.

The trip ended too soon. Faith thanked Pamela for the ride, then headed back to the manor.

Watson raced ahead of her until he was out of sight.

When Faith reached the building, she found her cat standing at the door, waiting for her to open it. No sooner had she done so than she was confronted by Marlene Russell, the manor's assistant manager.

Watson sprinted across the floor in the general direction of the library.

Marlene watched the black-and-white blur, then turned to Faith with an expression of mild distaste. For someone who worked in a business that catered to pet owners as well as book connoisseurs, Marlene was not exactly an animal lover, though she was always professional with the guests, both two-legged and four-legged. She checked her watch. "Taking a long lunch, are we?"

Faith looked at her own watch. Unless the time was off, she had fifteen minutes to spare, and she'd been hoping for a quick cup of clam chowder with Brooke in the kitchen before returning to work. "I've been chatting with a guest at the log cabin. Is someone waiting at the library?"

Marlene frowned. "Not that I'm aware of. But we're expecting the guests to begin arriving any minute. And you should be at your post."

As prickly as Marlene could be, she was remarkable at her job, taking it seriously and expecting others to exhibit the same dedication.

But Faith had the feeling that this admonishment was about something more. Ever since Faith and Wolfe had started dating, Marlene had seemed to disapprove, and since she could hardly say anything to Wolfe, her employer, Marlene occasionally took out her frustration on Faith.

Faith could understand. It was an unusual situation. Marlene was basically good-hearted, but she had a rather rigid nature as a result of some past mistakes. Faith had found that the best way to handle Marlene was to keep the conversation on a friendly, professional level to avoid setting her off.

"I'm headed back to the library now," Faith said evenly. It was a good thing she'd eaten a hearty breakfast. Brooke's undoubtedly delicious soup would have to wait.

2

An hour later, Wolfe entered the library with a briefcase in his hand. The afternoon sun streamed in through the French doors and glinted off the silver in his salt-and-pepper hair.

Faith smiled when he approached her desk. "This is a nice surprise."

He grinned back at her, his blue eyes bright. "I couldn't leave without saying goodbye."

"I didn't realize you had a trip planned," Faith said.

The Jaxon family businesses frequently required Wolfe to travel around the country and even across the globe. As the family member in charge of overseeing their shipping company as well as some of their other endeavors, like the manor's literary retreats, he spent quite a bit of time on the road.

He set the case down and took her hand. "It's a last-minute trip to New York, but I would rather stay here. With you."

Faith felt her heart flutter, as it so often did these days. She would miss him during his absence. "I wish you could stay too. But I have plenty of work to do, and guests are already arriving."

Wolfe squeezed her hand. "I'm sure the retreat will keep you busy."

Watson jumped down from a chair in front of the fireplace where he'd been napping and sauntered over to greet Wolfe. He rubbed against Wolfe's pant leg, then twined around his ankles, purring loudly. The cat raised his head and offered his chin for a scratching.

Wolfe released Faith's hand and bent down to comply. "I'm counting on you to keep this one out of trouble, okay?"

Watson collapsed on the floor in front of him and sprawled out with his vulnerable underside exposed.

The cat clearly approved of Faith's relationship with Wolfe. What would she have done if Watson, an excellent judge of character, hadn't liked Wolfe? Faith was rather glad she hadn't had to put the question to a test.

"There's no one here at the moment," Faith said. "Shall I walk you to your car?"

"I was hoping you would." Wolfe straightened and held out his arm.

Watson followed as they left the library and went out to the driveway.

Before they reached Wolfe's car, a purple limousine pulled up and stopped. Today was certainly the day for unusual vehicles.

Faith glanced at Wolfe.

He shrugged.

A young man hopped out of the driver's side. He was dressed in a purple sequined tuxedo, a matching vest, and a chauffeur's hat. An iridescent pocket square, a sparkly stickpin in his lapel, and a pair of blindingly white gloves accented his three-piece suit. The young man hurried to the back door and opened it with a flourish.

If Faith had been surprised by the car and its driver, she was positively stunned by the passenger. A tall woman dressed in a shimmering peacock-blue evening gown emerged from the limo. Her face was obscured by a heavy black veil over a wide-brimmed hat, and her hands and arms were covered with long black satin gloves.

But the biggest shock of all was the huge snake draped around the woman's neck. The reptile was at least ten feet long. Its skin was a light lilac color, and an orange-diamond pattern was interspersed with irregular pale-yellow markings along its length. The snake's eyes were pink, like those of an albino rabbit.

Faith had never seen anything quite like it before. And she wasn't particularly enjoying seeing it now.

Watson pressed against Faith's leg. Whether it was for Faith's comfort or his own, she couldn't tell.

The woman took a few long strides toward them. She gave the

snake a luxurious stroke, and the animal's body moved along with her hand.

The snake's tongue flicked out, then retreated back into its horrifying mouth.

Wolfe cleared his throat, stepped forward, and offered the woman his hand.

Faith admired his calm demeanor as he stood within striking distance of the snake. She wasn't sure she could have done the same if it had been asked of her.

"Welcome to Castleton Manor. I'm Wolfe Jaxon, one of the co-owners."

"Thank you. Some people know me as Fiona Perkins, but perhaps far more will recognize me as The Fantastical Fiona," the woman said in a husky, theatrical voice.

Faith stared at the woman in surprise. The Fantastical Fiona was a world-famous magician who had retired from public life a number of years ago after a trick involving a flaming cabinet had gone terribly wrong and she had become trapped inside.

She had attended one of Fiona's performances, but she would not have recognized her today because of the heavy veil. She could only imagine what the veil and gloves were covering and immediately felt sympathy for this poor woman.

"I'm so glad that you could join us," Wolfe said. "Unfortunately, you're catching me right as I'm leaving on a business trip."

"What a shame," Fiona intoned. "I assume there is someone else left in charge for the writers retreat?"

"We have a very capable assistant manager, Marlene Russell, who is in charge of our day-to-day operations." Wolfe turned to Faith. "You can also count on our librarian, Faith Newberry, while you're staying with us."

Faith held out her hand to Fiona. "It's a pleasure to meet you. Please don't hesitate to ask for anything you need."

Fiona shook her hand. "I may take you up on that. I would love a guided tour of the manor's famous library."

"Then please stop in anytime during business hours. I'll be happy to show you around." Faith hoped that her voice did not betray her nerves. Her gaze kept drifting from Fiona's veil to the snake draped around her shoulders.

Faith had a soft spot for most creatures. She had met all sorts of unusual pets during her time as the manor librarian and had thoroughly enjoyed most of them. But she couldn't feel genuinely enthusiastic about this snake. Especially a snake that was not contained in any sort of enclosure.

Surely Fiona had brought a cage with her. Or perhaps she'd already made arrangements with the manor's pet spa. A creature like that was unlikely to curl up in Fiona's bed at night, as Watson often did with Faith. She shivered at the thought that she might be wrong about the assumption.

"I'm sure that Gunther and I will enjoy ourselves immensely." Fiona stroked the snake again with her gloved hand. "We've been looking forward to our visit to the manor for some time."

Faith nodded to the chauffeur, who had closed the limousine's door and was now retrieving bags from the spacious trunk. She didn't see a cage among the luggage. "Is Gunther your driver?"

Fiona gave a hoarse laugh. "Heavens, no. Gunther is my snake." She reached down and lifted the snake's head close to her face.

Faith repressed a shudder as the serpent flicked its tongue over the dense netting of Fiona's veil.

"Gunther seems to be quite an exotic specimen," Wolfe said smoothly, without a trace of the discomfort Faith was feeling. "I've never seen coloring quite like that on a snake before."

"He is rather a special creature," Fiona said. "Gunther is a lavender albino reticulated python. They are not the most common of pets, even among reptile enthusiasts."

"He makes quite an impression," Faith said.

"That is precisely what he is meant to do." Fiona lowered the snake's head once more.

Just then the young man in the sequined tuxedo approached, carrying two large suitcases and a stack of hatboxes.

"And speaking of those who make an impression," Fiona said, "this is my driver and assistant, Cody James."

"I'd shake your hand, but I'm a little tied up at the moment," the young man said.

"Cody has expressed an interest in stage magic. I have been mentoring him in some of the finer points of illusion and showmanship," Fiona said, gesturing toward his sequined suit. "And he's agreed to put up with Gunther and me."

"I enjoy every minute of it," Cody responded.

"What a great setup for you, to be tutored by someone so accomplished," Faith told him.

"Are you familiar with my act?" Fiona asked, stepping closer.

Faith recoiled inwardly from the nearness of the enormous snake but managed to hold her ground. "I saw one of your last performances in Boston some years ago. The show was absolutely astonishing."

"That's very kind of you to say," Fiona replied. "It's nice to know that someone still remembers me after all this time."

"I would be very surprised if anyone who had seen you perform could ever forget you. Your stage presence was mesmerizing." Faith wasn't exaggerating. She had been truly amazed by Fiona's performance.

"You are too sweet," Fiona said, then leaned in even closer. "Shall I let you in on a little secret?"

Faith realized she was holding her breath. She forced herself to exhale silently before speaking. "I would be honored."

"I am quite sure that what I plan to write in my memoir will create even more of a stir than my farewell tour ever did," Fiona said, then turned to Cody. "Wouldn't you agree?"

"I make it a policy to agree with you about everything," Cody said with a grin. "But right now I would like to put the luggage away in your room. And I'm sure Gunther is getting hungry. We didn't feed him before we left."

As if to agree, Gunther raised his head in Faith's direction and fixed his gaze on her with one of his lidless eyes.

Faith was grateful that both Wolfe and Watson stood close at her side. She felt slightly faint as the huge snake weaved his head back and forth slowly.

"Whatever else happens, we can't allow Gunther to get hungry," Fiona said. "We should go inside and check in." With that, the statuesque lady strode off in the direction of the manor, leaving Cody struggling to keep up under the heavy burden of the luggage.

Wolfe and Faith stared after them.

"It's shaping up to be quite a week," Wolfe finally said. "I'm sorry to have to miss it."

"I'm sorry too," Faith said. "I wonder what the rest of the guests and the staff will make of The Fantastical Fiona and her reptile sidekick."

"They're quite a showstopping pair, aren't they?" Wolfe said.

"That's one way to describe it," Faith said. "I think I'll feel far more comfortable if Gunther spends most of the time curled up in a terrarium rather than draped around her neck."

"Are you afraid of snakes?" Wolfe asked, his voice warm with concern.

Faith was no fan of snakes, but she was no helpless female either. "I'm sure Fiona wouldn't have brought Gunther unless he was well-behaved. There's probably nothing to worry about." She checked her watch. "You'd best get going before you're late for your flight."

Wolfe nodded. "I'll call you soon to see how things are going." He gave her a light kiss, then hurried toward his car and the waiting driver.

With a heavy heart, Faith watched Wolfe leave. She was always sorry to see him go, but this time her sadness was mixed with trepidation.

Watson again seemed to sense her discomfort. He placed a paw gently on her leg.

She scooped him into her arms and cradled him against her neck. "I can't imagine anyone wanting a snake when they could have a pet as soft and cuddly as you."

Watson purred loudly.

But Faith didn't feel her usual sense of calm at his show of attention. She was uneasy about the presence of the enormous serpent at the manor, but that wasn't the only reason.

Had she simply imagined it, or had there been an underlying tone of menace in Fiona's promise that her memoir would cause a stir?

3

It was clear that his human was upset. The cat wasn't exactly at ease with a large reptile lurking about in his domain either.

And now the nice man had left them, and he had no one to share responsibility for his person. He had come to rely on the man as a source of comfort and protection. It was a good thing he knew what to do on his own.

His human was reluctant to enter the building, so he purred loudly and encouragingly. He sensed her heart rate slow, as it always did when he comforted her.

He focused on the hallway in front of them. The reptile was nowhere in sight. Instead, more unfamiliar humans and an unpleasant-looking canine stood between him and the room with all the books.

The dog noticed the cat immediately, but the pair of humans paid him no mind.

As his person approached the others, he could sense that the dog was not happy to see him. However, this was the cat's domain, and the canine would need to be told its place.

The cat hopped down from his human's embrace and crossed the hallway to make his ownership of the space clear. He stopped a few feet from the animal and sat down.

The dog growled low in its throat. The pathetic animal tried to lunge at the cat, but one of the humans, the male and the older of the two, yanked on the canine's leash, stopping it. The dog strained forward, still growling.

But the cat remained out of reach. He lifted his paw and began to carefully groom it to show his lack of fear. This served to infuriate the dog even more.

The canine obviously thought he could frighten him away, but the cat had no intention of relinquishing the field of battle.

"Athena does not care for cats," the portly gentleman explained, gesturing to his English bulldog. The fringe of white hair on his head reminded Faith of dandelion fluff. "Nor do I. I hope it will not make a nuisance of itself."

"I'm sorry to hear that," Faith said. "My cat roams freely about the manor most of the time. Watson is well-behaved, and he comes to work with me every day and often makes himself at home in the library."

She bent down and picked up Watson again. This did not stop the dog from growling, but Faith felt calmer knowing her cat was out of harm's way, even though Watson had consistently shown that he was quite capable of taking care of himself.

"Then the pair of you will have to make the best of it now, won't you?" the woman said to the man and his dog. Her dark hair was streaked with gray and was scraped back tightly into a bun. Her face was long and thin and completely devoid of makeup. Loosely draped over her thin shoulders was a blue cardigan held together at the throat with a handsome cameo brooch.

The man did not respond.

"You cannot expect to have everything your own way when there are so many pets here," the woman continued. She arched her eyebrows and seemed prepared to counter any argument from her companion.

The man seemed annoyed by the woman's reprimand and allowed Athena a little slack on her lead.

The dog advanced closer to Faith's ankles and growled even more loudly.

Watson snuggled back against Faith. She wasn't sure if he was frightened or if he was attempting to protect her.

"I suppose we shall have to tolerate it, then," the man said with a sigh.

"I hope that we can put this little incident behind us," Faith said, trying to smooth things over. She smiled and introduced herself. "Please enjoy your stay at Castleton."

"Thank you," the woman said. "I'm certain that we will all have a wonderful time. I love libraries, and I hear this one is exceptional."

"It definitely is," Faith said. "Feel free to stop by anytime. I'd be happy to show you around. Are you both here for the writers retreat?"

"Oh no, I'm not a writer," the woman said. "I'm here with the judge as his private nurse. I'm Diana Marsden."

Diana had excellent posture and a capable manner, and Faith could easily imagine her dressed in the nurse's uniform of days gone by. A white dress and a starched, neat cap would have suited her slim frame and small face.

"I'm the writer." The man extended his hand to Faith. "Judge Jerome Davidson. I've been working on my memoir for some time, and I jumped at the chance to attend this retreat."

Faith shook his hand. "You sound devoted to your craft," she said, noting the enthusiastic gleam in the judge's eyes.

"I most certainly am," the judge said pompously. "With the insight I have into the legal system, I consider it my civic duty to share my story."

"I wish you had a bit less concern with your duty to others and more for yourself," Diana said. She turned to Faith. "I urged him to cancel this trip, but he wouldn't hear of it."

"That's why I employ you," the judge muttered.

"I didn't want him to risk it, but he insisted he would attend the retreat with or without me," Diana continued, ignoring the judge's comment. "I finally decided the best way to keep him healthy was to come with him."

Faith wondered what sort of health concerns might have kept

the judge from visiting a relaxing environment like the one at the manor.

She didn't need to wonder long. Judge Davidson was apparently eager to share his medical history with a total stranger. "It was my gallbladder. I had to have it out. The doctor said that if I took the proper precautions, I was in the clear to attend this event."

Diana huffed. "It's easy for the surgeon to say since he isn't the one keeping an eye on you day in and day out."

"You're a worrywart," the judge retorted.

"It isn't only his gallbladder," Diana said to Faith. "He has a serious chronic heart condition, and his case was more complicated than that of most patients."

"The surgeon said he couldn't see any reason why I should have to miss all the fun on account of a fairly minor procedure," the judge said. "Besides, you've watched out for me long enough to know how well I bounce back."

Diana nodded. "He was on his feet with time to spare. In the end, I had to agree he seemed up to the trip, so here we are."

"I'm sure you'll make a wonderful addition to the group," Faith said, changing the subject before even more of the judge's private history was revealed.

"I'll drop by the library later," Diana said to Faith, then took the judge's arm. "Let's get you up to your room. You've had enough activity for a few hours, and I need to check your blood pressure."

As Faith watched them turn to leave, she felt Watson's body relax in her arms. She hadn't noticed that his muscles had been taut, as if he were ready to spring. He twitched his whiskers ever so slightly. She couldn't shake the feeling that Watson did not like the judge.

She had to agree with her cat. Perhaps it was the judge's tone or the way he spoke to his employee. He certainly acted self-important, which was a bit off-putting.

She felt rather sorry for both the nurse and the bulldog—although

Diana seemed to hold her own with the judge, and Athena hadn't exactly been pleasant thus far. She could not imagine what it would be like to live with or work for this querulous man.

Before the judge and the nurse were out of sight, a couple strolled down the hall toward them. The man was tall with dark hair and a goatee. He was dressed casually in khakis and a polo shirt. The woman wore a gauzy sundress and a large quantity of gold jewelry. Cascades of auburn curls fell to her shoulders and framed her heart-shaped face. She cradled a black-and-tan guinea pig in her arms.

The man hurried over to the judge and clapped him soundly on the back. "Jerry, you old dog. I knew you'd find a way to make it to the retreat, even if you were on your deathbed."

The judge glowered at the man, and Athena barked ferociously.

Diana pursed her thin lips but said nothing.

"I take my commitment to my memoir project very seriously," the judge said. "Whereas some are mere dilettantes."

"See, sweetheart, I told you Jerry would try to provoke me," the man said to his companion, then faced the judge again. "You want to watch that, buddy. It's not good for the old ticker."

"I would hardly take health advice from a builder," the judge scoffed. "And a shady one at that, Mr. Hoyle."

"So you keep telling me every time I end up coming before your bench," the man replied.

The judge harrumphed.

"Christina, my love," the man continued, "you finally have the opportunity to meet the single biggest thorn in my side."

Athena advanced toward the woman and sniffed at her high heels.

Christina lifted her guinea pig out of the dog's reach. "You must be Judge Davidson. I've heard a great deal about you from Terrence."

"You have me at a disadvantage, ma'am," the judge said. "You know who I am, but I have no idea who you are."

"How rude of me," Terrence said. "My wife never accompanies

me to court, so of course you haven't met her. Allow me to introduce my better half, Christina Hoyle." He turned to his spouse with a broad smile that exposed overly white teeth.

"Don't forget Prunella," Christina said, holding out the guinea pig.

Athena growled again.

Christina pulled the guinea pig back against her chest.

"At least one of you has the good sense not to get hauled up before the court." The judge glared at Terrence, then tugged on Athena's leash and marched down the hall.

Diana hurried after him.

"It's so easy to rile that guy up." Terrence laughed. "This week is going to be even more enjoyable than I had expected."

"I wish you wouldn't say things like that. People might take you seriously." Christina glanced nervously at Faith, then shifted the little guinea pig in her arms slightly until she held it directly in front of her, almost like a shield.

Prunella didn't seem particularly fierce, so Faith wasn't sure how much help she'd be in a dangerous situation. The silly thought didn't do much to dispel Faith's concern over the decidedly cool atmosphere that was already descending over this retreat—and it hadn't even officially started yet.

"My wife worries too much about what other people think," Terrence said as he noticed Faith. He introduced himself, even though Faith had already learned his name, and extended a hand to her.

"I'm Faith Newberry, the librarian here." She shook his hand, noting the strength of his grip and the calluses on his fingers. Despite Terrence's easy smile, Faith couldn't help but sense that something far less friendly simmered just below the surface. He had taken too much delight in provoking the judge.

"Oh, I can't wait to see the famous library," Christina said.

"It's magnificent," Faith responded. "Are you both attending the writers retreat?"

"He's here to write." Christina rested a perfectly manicured hand on her husband's arm. "And I'm planning to relax in our suite and at the spa. When I heard that Prunella could come too, I couldn't believe my good fortune."

"I hope to see you and Prunella often during your stay," Faith said, smiling at the adorable little creature.

Watson sniffed the air as if he had caught the scent of something interesting.

Faith hoped he would not prove to be too curious about the newcomer. She had a feeling Christina was very attached to her pet and would not welcome any attention to it from her cat.

"Since you work here, maybe you could answer a question for me," Terrence said.

"I can try," Faith said.

"Like the judge said, I'm a building contractor," Terrence went on. "I'm quite interested in places like this. How big is the manor?"

"There really is no place like Castleton Manor," Faith answered. "It's sixty thousand square feet, and it has twenty-nine bedrooms and thirty-four bathrooms."

Terrence let out a low whistle. "Impressive. It's hard to believe that a place this massive was built as a private home. No one makes them this grand anymore."

"I hope the manor is big enough for both Judge Davidson and you," Christina said, raising an eyebrow. She turned to Faith. "My husband and the judge have a long history, and none of it is good."

After witnessing the conversation between the judge and Terrence, Faith wasn't surprised by the news.

"Having the judge around doesn't make me the least bit uncomfortable," Terrence said, then emitted a deep, rumbling laugh. "But it will be a lot of fun to watch how much it bothers him."

"It serves him right for being such a snob," Christina said.

"I expect he doesn't like to think that he could be caught fraternizing with a common thug like me." Terrence held out his arm to his wife. "Let's check in and then go up to our suite."

As Faith watched the couple walk down the hallway, she wondered why Terrence had been in court before the judge—and more than once.

With the judge's heart problems and Terrence's clear intent to provoke him, Faith feared this retreat was already doomed.

The next morning Faith woke early but stayed in bed, luxuriating in the warmth from the quilt her grandmother had made many years ago, with Watson curled up beside her.

The former gardener's cottage, which was a fantastic perk of her job, was as cozy as the manor was ornate. She had to admit that she preferred her simple surroundings, although she wouldn't want to go too simple—like the log cabin on the edge of the property. Running water was a definite advantage of modern life.

Watson leaped off the bed and headed for the doorway, then glanced at her over his shoulder.

Faith took one more moment to savor the peace and quiet before throwing back the covers. "All right, Rumpy. Let's get some breakfast."

The cat led the way to the kitchen and stood expectantly in front of his food and water bowls.

Faith dutifully filled them both. On top of the dry food, like a fishy cherry on top, she placed a tunaroon—Watson's favorite treat, made by Faith's good friend Midge Foster. Midge sold treats for all kinds of animals at her Happy Tails Gourmet Bakery in downtown Lighthouse Bay.

Watson ate the morsel slowly as if savoring it, then crunched away on his kibble.

For herself, Faith made a cup of coffee and a piece of cinnamon toast. She briefly considered scrambling an egg, but a look at the clock on the stove told her she'd better pass.

After eating her breakfast, she made quick work of getting ready for the day. Soon she was striding toward the manor, Watson trotting ahead of her on the path. He probably had plans for a long nap in one of the chairs by the fireplace in the library.

When she reached the Great Hall Gallery, Faith paused at the sound of raised voices. Even from a distance, Faith could feel the tension crackling in the air.

Watson stopped suddenly at her side.

Diana stood with Fiona and Cody in front of the statue of Dame Agatha Christie. The little group was so absorbed in their conversation that they took no notice of Faith or her cat.

"What are you talking about?" Fiona demanded.

"I was horrified when I went into the conservatory this morning and saw a snake in there." Diana shook a finger right in front of Fiona's face. "I asked the front desk clerk who that animal belonged to, and she told me it was yours."

Fiona straightened to an even more considerable height. Once again, the magician was dressed in a flamboyant outfit that would have been more appropriate onstage. Her gown was encrusted with silver sequins, and her face was shaded by a large hat covered by a burgundy veil. Long black gloves still covered her arms from the tips of her fingers all the way up to her elbows.

Faith was relieved to see that instead of the live python, a decidedly inanimate scarlet feather boa was wrapped around her neck.

Cody inched closer to his employer's side. Today he was more plainly dressed than he had been yesterday. He wore a tailored black suit and shiny dress shoes. With his broad shoulders and sandy-blond hair, he resembled a professional athlete or a model in a sportswear catalog.

"That is correct," Fiona said, tipping her head to stare down at the far more diminutive woman. "Though I cannot see what it has to do with you."

"It has everything to do with me because it concerns my patient," Diana said, her words echoing in the cavernous space. "I can't imagine what it would do to the judge if he were to stumble across a snake haphazardly left in the conservatory."

"There's nothing haphazard about it," Cody chimed in. "I made sure that Gunther was properly secured in his terrarium."

Diana crossed her arms over her chest. "Secured or not, an enormous boa constrictor is in a public area where any guest might come upon it without notice."

"Gunther is a reticulated python, not a boa constrictor," Fiona clarified. "And say what you like, but I have been told that all pets are welcome here at Castleton Manor."

"In my opinion, they shouldn't be," Diana argued. "Or they should at least be kept in the kennels, where they belong. It's not fair for the other guests. My patient has an absolute horror of snakes."

"So do many people," Fiona retorted. "But that still doesn't make it my problem."

"The snake's presence creates a health hazard," Diana insisted. "The judge has a chronic heart condition, and encountering your pet is likely to cause a serious incident."

"My pet has every right to be here," Fiona continued, her voice rising several decibels. "Nothing you have to say will change my mind. Perhaps you should instruct your patient to stay out of the conservatory."

"You'll be responsible if Judge Davidson has a heart attack because you didn't remove that snake from where he might happen upon it," Diana warned, a note of genuine distress in her voice.

Faith felt Watson stiffen beside her. She glanced down at him and saw that his ears were pricked up. He was on high alert.

"Did you say Judge Davidson?" Cody asked, an astonished look flickering across his face.

"Yes, Judge Jerome Davidson," Diana replied. "I'm his private nurse, and I must insist on conditions that will keep him as healthy as possible."

Fiona turned to Cody. "Didn't I mention to you that he would be here?" The angry tone in her voice had been replaced by one of amusement.

Faith was surprised that another guest knew the judge. She hoped Fiona wasn't trying to provoke the man as Terrence had attempted to do.

Cody scowled. "I definitely would have remembered."

"While I understand you may have reason to bear Judge Davidson some ill will," Diana said, placing both hands on her hips, "I cannot imagine you would really wish to contribute to his health troubles."

"In the past, my health difficulties were of no concern to him whatsoever," Fiona said.

Diana's face softened. "Surely you do not want to be responsible for harming another human being."

"I think you presume too much there," Cody told her.

"Yes, my assistant is correct," Fiona said. "The fact is that I am not much of a fan of human beings in general. As to the judge in particular, I would be delighted if he turned up his toes." She whirled around and strode away, her long gown flowing out behind her.

Diana gasped. She faced Cody, clearly shocked. "She didn't actually mean that, did she?"

"What she meant was that Gunther would be doing the world a tremendous favor if he managed to cause Judge Davidson's untimely demise," Cody said, glowering at her.

Faith shivered at the young man's expression. She couldn't help but think he shared Fiona's opinion.

The clock had just struck one thirty when Diana walked into the library.

Faith glanced up from the bookcase where she was shelving a detective novel that one of the housekeepers had checked out. The library had been quiet, as all the writers groups were meeting in the dining room for a seminar.

Out of the corner of her eye, she noticed Watson lift his head to regard Diana. He was curled up on a chair in front of the fireplace. The cat squinted slightly, then lowered his head and returned to his nap.

Faith guessed Watson was relieved that the irritable bulldog wasn't accompanying the nurse. She approached Diana. "Is there something I can do for you?"

"I'd like to find something to read while the judge is in the seminar," Diana said. "It seems like a good time to brush up on the classics. Do you have any recommendations?"

"Certainly." Faith smiled as she led Diana to one of the bookshelves and pointed out a few of her favorites.

While Faith was checking out Diana's selection, a woman entered the library.

Faith excused herself to the nurse, then went over to greet the newcomer and introduce herself. "Is there something I can assist you with?"

"I only wanted to see the library that I've heard so much about." The woman gave Faith a wide smile. A large dimple adorned each of her apple-shaped cheeks, and freckles speckled her pert button nose. With her honey-colored hair pulled back in a ponytail and her coordinated pink tracksuit and matching running shoes, she was the picture of health.

"Thanks again," Diana said to Faith. She rushed out of the room.

Faith didn't even have a chance to respond. *Why the sudden hurry?*

"It's an impressive collection," the woman said. Her gaze traveled around the room, her eyes wide with appreciation.

Faith never tired of seeing the awe on the guests' faces when they first took in the remarkable library. "You must be one of the guests arriving for the retreat."

The woman nodded. "Janine Peters."

"Are you related to Philip Peters, the architect?" Faith asked.

"Philip is my husband." She smiled. "We're both thrilled to be here."

"Your husband's done a marvelous job on the log cabin," Faith told her. "It makes such a delightful addition to the grounds."

"He's really thrown himself into the project," Janine said. "It's the first time he's ever designed something quite like that, and he's been so excited to see it completed."

"Are you attending the retreat yourself, or are you here simply to enjoy your husband's handiwork?" Faith asked.

"A bit of both. I'm going to the sessions as a writer." A slight furrow appeared between Janine's eyes. "Since my husband has been so busy with several projects and we've barely seen each other lately, I thought it would be a great way to spend time together."

Faith gave her a reassuring smile. "Our guests often tell us that the manor is an ideal place to reconnect with important people in their lives. I'm sure you'll have a wonderful time."

Janine bit her lip, and the furrow on her brow deepened.

Was there more to Janine's concerns than too much time spent apart from her husband?

"I hope so," Janine finally said. "But I'm not sure how smoothly things will go with this particular mix of guests."

Ever since meeting the judge and learning about past grievances between him and at least two other guests, Faith had been concerned about the very same thing. She was surprised to hear Janine was worrying about it too.

"Do you already know some of the other guests?" Faith asked.

Janine sighed. "Unfortunately, I do. And more importantly, so does Philip."

"It sounds as though there may have been a disagreement," Faith said carefully. "I hope it was a minor one."

"If Philip manages to stay away from both Terrence Hoyle and Judge Davidson, things should turn out okay. Otherwise, I'm afraid

I'm going to wish that we had never heard of Castleton Manor."

"That sounds serious," Faith said. Did everyone have a bone to pick with the judge?

"Not too long ago, Philip was hired by Terrence Hoyle and his construction company to design a gated community."

"I'm guessing it didn't go as planned," Faith prompted.

"Terrence decided not to pay Philip," Janine explained. "I wouldn't put it past him to have planned not to pay all along."

"I can see how that would lead to some strain," Faith said.

"It wasn't just that. The dispute resulted in a nasty court case."

"What do you mean?" Faith could see where this was going, and Janine's next words confirmed her suspicions.

"The case went up before Judge Davidson, and he found for Philip." Strangely, Janine did not sound happy about her husband winning the lawsuit.

Faith knew that people were often disgruntled by their interactions with the legal system. After all, there was always a winner and a loser. But if Philip had been victorious, she couldn't see how he would have a reason to resent the judge.

She regarded Janine. "I understand that it would be awkward, but surely Philip can't have a dispute with both the judge and Terrence if he won the case, can he?"

"You would think that, wouldn't you?" Janine said. "Philip was seeking punitive damages in addition to the design fees he was owed. He ended up losing a lot of sleep and even clients over the whole mess. And then Judge Davidson awarded him one single dollar after all those months of anguish."

Faith thought that sounded almost mean-spirited. Not that she was an expert on the legal world, but she could definitely see how someone would find a merely symbolic ruling disappointing. She had to agree with Janine that it seemed likely there was bound to be hostility between these three guests during the retreat.

"I'm sorry to hear that," Faith said. "Your husband's work on the log cabin has been extraordinary, and I hope he remains in business for many years to come."

"Thank you." Janine gave her a weak smile. "Perhaps this week will help him to put it all behind him. The log cabin project was the first thing he's seemed excited about since the ruling."

"Then let's both hope for the very best," Faith said. "Now are you sure there isn't something I can help you with? Would you like a tour of the library?"

"Well, I am interested in a book of short essays and magazine articles that Laura Ingalls Wilder wrote during the course of her career," Janine said. "I can't remember the name of it, though."

"Do you mean *Little House in the Ozarks*?"

Janine gasped. "How did you know that right off the top of your head?"

"I brushed up on her works in order to advise on the log cabin and to prepare for the retreat. We have a copy right over here." Faith led the way to a small alcove on the far side of the library where she had gathered the Laura Ingalls Wilder books and materials.

Before she could pull the requested volume from the shelf, Cody burst into the room and rushed up to them. "I'm sorry to interrupt, but it's an emergency. Gunther is missing."

5

Panic washed over Faith. Of all the pets that could be lost, why did it have to be the reticulated python?

"The last time I saw Gunther, he was draped across Fiona's shoulders when she first arrived," Faith said. Hadn't she overheard Cody telling Diana that the snake was in his terrarium in the conservatory?

"You haven't seen him since then?" Cody pressed, his voice trembling. "Not with any of the other guests?"

Faith knew Janine was listening, and she didn't want to alarm the guests. "Just a moment, Cody. Please let me finish up with Mrs. Peters so she can get on with enjoying her day."

Cody nodded.

Faith swiftly searched through the collection of material written by or about Laura Ingalls Wilder, found the copy of *Little House in the Ozarks*, and checked it out for Janine.

Fortunately, Janine didn't seem to want to hang around, because she thanked Faith, took her book, and left the library. Perhaps she wasn't the curious sort. Faith could only hope she was also discreet.

As soon as Janine was gone, Faith turned back to Cody. "What exactly is going on?"

"I was in the conservatory to check on Gunther, but he wasn't there."

Faith felt slightly dizzy. She knew that Diana was convinced that being surprised by the reticulated python could give Judge Davidson a heart attack, but the snake could pose other sorts of dangers to the rest of the guests as well.

How big would a python need to be before it could harm someone? Gunther was huge. She was pretty sure he could do damage if he was so inclined, although she didn't know enough about pythons to identify what form that might take. Were they venomous? She thought they were the kind of snake that squeezed its prey to death, but she didn't like the creatures enough to have studied them, so she couldn't be sure.

Faith chided herself for letting her imagination run wild. She had to pull herself together and stop imagining the worst-case scenario. She took a few deep breaths before asking, "Have you started searching for Gunther yet?"

"Of course I have," Cody snapped. "He's not in Fiona's room, he's not around her neck, and he's not in the pet spa."

"Did you ask Fiona about him?" Faith said.

Cody shook his head emphatically. "Fiona has quite a temper even under the best of circumstances. I didn't want to upset her. And she definitely would be upset if she found out about this. She loves Gunther more than anything else in the world."

"I noticed she seemed very protective of him," Faith said.

"I wouldn't want to think about what would happen to somebody who endangered Gunther," Cody said in a tone that sent a chill up Faith's spine.

Faith was taken aback for a moment. Then she cleared her throat. "I can see why you would be worried. The judge isn't the only one who might not react well to a snake slithering around."

The manor was not only large, but it was full of nooks and crannies. There were so many places a snake could hide if it had somehow escaped. Gunther could be under furniture, in a cupboard, or even in the ventilation shafts. Faith shuddered. She didn't even want to consider the number of secret passages and tunnels tucked away throughout the vast building.

"I hadn't thought about the reactions of the other guests," Cody admitted. "My mind was completely taken up with worrying about what to say to my boss."

"I understand your concern about telling Fiona," Faith said. "But someone needs to report it to Ms. Russell, the assistant manager."

"I guess you're right," Cody said. His shoulders sagged, and his posture drooped. "Will you do that while I tell Fiona? I guess there's no avoiding it."

Faith nodded. She suspected that Marlene wasn't going to be any happier about the news than Fiona. But one look at Cody's face told Faith that she was getting the better deal.

"Is it really as bad as that?" Faith asked gently. "An animal that size can't stay hidden for too long, can it?"

Cody's forehead was creased with worry. "If Fiona discovers I'm responsible for losing Gunther, she may just kill me."

Faith found Marlene in the salon giving instructions to a staff member about an event planned later in the month.

While much of the manor was made up of massive rooms and awe-inspiring architecture, the salon had a cozy, comforting feel. With its wood floors and pale walls, the room invited guests and staff to linger within it. Faith supposed this was as good a place as any to break the news.

She waited until Marlene had finished her conversation and the other staff member had left the room.

Marlene gave Faith her most imperious gaze. "There isn't anything wrong in the library, is there?"

"No. It concerns a guest," Faith answered. "Or rather a guest's pet."

"What is it?" Marlene asked, glancing at her watch.

Faith took a deep breath. "The reticulated python that belongs to Fiona Perkins has been misplaced."

Marlene gasped. "You mean that creature is slithering around loose in the manor?"

"I don't know," Faith admitted. "Fiona's assistant, Cody, told me the snake isn't in his terrarium."

"Did he check with Ms. Perkins?" Marlene asked. "She seemed to enjoy wearing the snake around her neck. Perhaps she took him."

"Yes, and he told me that Gunther isn't with her," Faith said. "I thought you should know immediately."

"I'll call animal control and ask them to send someone over right away," Marlene said, pulling her cell phone from her tailored jacket pocket.

Faith waited while Marlene got through to the authorities and explained the situation. Midge would have been someone else to call for help. Not only did Midge own the pet bakery, but she was the manor's concierge veterinarian. However, Midge was currently on vacation.

Marlene hung up and turned her attention to Faith once more. "They're sending someone as soon as possible. Apparently, the animal control officer is on the other side of town responding to a call about a potentially rabid fox."

"Did they say if it would take long?" Faith asked.

"They couldn't say for sure." Marlene shook her head. "It seems a rabid fox in a residential neighborhood poses a greater threat than a loose python."

"Do you think we should notify the guests to keep an eye out just to be on the safe side?" Faith asked.

"I don't want to spread unnecessary terror, but I suppose it would be better to let them know than to risk having someone come upon the snake unaware," Marlene said. "I'll make the rounds and tell the guests and the staff."

"I can stop in at the kitchen to inform Brooke," Faith offered.

"Then I'll need you to wait at the front desk to fill in the animal control officer when he arrives," Marlene said. "I'll have my hands full mobilizing the staff and keeping the guests calm."

Now if Faith could only keep herself calm.

Faith went downstairs to the kitchen. In the basement, space was tighter but far from claustrophobic. The walls of the corridors were mostly plain with well-worn wood floors.

When Faith entered the kitchen, Brooke was standing at the stove, stirring something in an enormous copper pot.

Brooke glanced up and smiled. "Are you here for a snack?" She set the spoon down and wiped her hands on her apron. "I can put together some cheese and crackers with some Macoun apple slices."

"That sounds delicious," Faith said, "but I don't have time."

Brooke peered at her. "What is it? You look worried."

"One of the guest's pets has gone missing."

"Oh no! Which one?"

"Gunther, Fiona's enormous python," Faith answered. If the situation had not been so serious, she realized she might have been amused that a magician's pet seemed to have pulled a vanishing act.

Brooke's eyes widened. "A snake loose in the manor? Are we in any danger?"

"Well, we don't actually know that the snake is loose," Faith clarified. "But we don't know where he is right now. Animal control is on the way, but everyone needs to be on alert."

Brooke let out a low whistle. "Diva and Bling were acting strange this morning. I guess this explains it."

Brooke was convinced that her angelfish could spot a loser guy a mile away, and now it sounded like she believed they could make predictions about snakes. Faith wasn't as convinced of their amazing abilities, but she had to admit they had a fair track record of warning Brooke about bad dates.

"Snakes creep me out even when they're locked up in glass cages at the zoo," Brooke continued. "The idea that one is loose in the manor makes me more than a little jumpy."

"I'm not thrilled about it either," Faith agreed.

"Are you sure I can't tempt you with some comfort food?" Brooke asked. "Like a brownie?"

"Thanks, but I need to go," Faith said. "Before the animal control officer gets here, I'm going to take Watson to the cottage. I don't want him to be the one who finds Gunther."

"Good idea. Watson's an extraordinary cat, but I'd hate to see what would happen if he came face-to-face with a python."

Faith left Brooke and headed back to the library. She found Watson still napping on a chair in front of the fireplace.

"Would you like to go home and have a treat?" Faith asked him.

At the word *treat*, Watson perked up. He jumped off the chair and dashed to the door.

Faith laughed. "I'll take that as a yes."

When they arrived at the cottage, Faith set a tunaroon in his bowl. "Promise me that you'll stay here while I'm gone."

He blinked slowly, as if in agreement.

At least Faith hoped it was agreement. Watson was an intrepid explorer and could move with lightning speed, but she wasn't sure he was a match for a python.

Faith wondered if any of them was a match for such a beast.

6

Faith returned to the manor at the same time as the animal control officer pulled up in a white van. Relief washed over her. Surely this professional would know what to do, although she suspected that Cape Cod was not exactly a haven for exotic reptiles.

A tall, dark-haired man wearing a matching khaki shirt and trousers exited the vehicle. He held out his hand when he saw her. "I'm Roland Finnegan with animal control. I hear you have a snake problem."

Faith shook his hand. "I'm Faith Newberry, the librarian. Yes, we have a reticulated python on the loose, and we're not sure what to do." She ushered him toward the front door of the manor. "Naturally, we're concerned about our guests' safety."

"Can you describe the animal for me?"

Faith felt a knot in her stomach as she recalled the scene in front of the manor when Fiona had first arrived. She described Gunther as best she could.

Roland held the door open for her and followed her inside. He gave a low whistle. "This place is amazing. I've always wanted to see the interior, but I'm not really a bookish guy, and a lot of the animals I deal with—raccoons and such—don't belong in a pet spa." He chuckled.

Faith laughed too, which dispelled a bit of her stress. "You'd be surprised at some of the animals who have stayed here with their owners. We even had a hedgehog once," she added as she led him toward the conservatory.

"What about the python's size?" he asked.

"I would say he's at least ten feet long," Faith answered, remembering how the reptile had draped almost to the ground as it hung over Fiona's shoulders.

Roland nodded, glancing around as they walked. "Despite the size of this place, I'd say it's going to be hard for him to hide unless he's made his way outside somehow. Then we'll have a bigger problem."

Faith wasn't sure which would be worse—Gunther slithering around the manor or outdoors among the topiaries. Either way, an unsuspecting guest or pet could easily come into contact with him. "Just how dangerous is he?" she finally asked, feeling the knot in her stomach tighten again.

He looked her in the eye. "Fatal attacks by large snakes are very uncommon, but they're not entirely unprecedented."

"So we might all be at risk?" Faith asked. She had hoped that when the animal control officer arrived, he would chuckle kindly and reassure her that there was no way a pet python was anything to worry about. Instead, her conversation with him was making her even more nervous than before.

"Like I said, attacks on humans are rare," Roland replied. "Fatal attacks are even less common, but you should know that they have been known to happen."

Faith nodded.

"I'd like to start searching the manor and the grounds immediately," he said.

"Are there any precautions we should take?"

"The first thing to do is avoid panicking," Roland said. "Have you informed the guests to be on the lookout for the snake?"

"Ms. Russell, the assistant manager, has that under control," Faith said. "And she's assigning staff to investigate as well."

"Good. Has anyone reported seeing any sign of him? A trail visible in the nap of a carpet or something knocked off a table, perhaps?"

She should have thought of that. "Not that I know of, but we only learned he was missing a short time before we called you. I don't think anyone's had time to search very thoroughly yet."

"Please try not to worry. It is very rare for pythons to attack people," he repeated, clearly reading the anxiety on her face.

They reached the conservatory, and Faith escorted him inside.

The smell of damp earth and fragrant, tropical blossoms filled the moist, heavy air. Deep-red, trumpet-shaped flowers dangled from vines clinging to the window frames and ceiling beams.

In the far corner of the sun-drenched conservatory stood a large koi pond. A sparkling waterfall tumbled the full length of the adjacent wall, cascading neatly into the pond and filling the air with a pleasant splashing sound.

Overhead fans turned steadily, causing lush green leaves to wave in the breeze. Usually Faith loved the visual, but now all she could think was that any motion in the foliage from a slithering creature could easily be attributed to the ventilation.

Roland scanned the room. "This is exactly the kind of environment a cold-blooded reptile would like. Plenty of light and warmth."

"It's the last place he was seen," Faith said.

"Then it's a good place to start," Roland said. "I'll search for anything that might help us determine where the snake might have gone. Who was the last person to see the snake?"

"Cody James."

"I'd like to ask him a few questions too."

"Of course. I'll go find him." Faith left Roland in the conservatory. Her search for Cody didn't last long. She spotted him standing in front of the French doors in the Great Hall Gallery.

Faith assumed Cody would be frantically searching for Gunther, so she was surprised to see the young man juggling. Several red, green, and yellow balls flashed through the air in front of him in a complicated pattern.

When Cody noticed Faith, he let each ball drop into one hand, then made them disappear within the depths of his suit. "I hope it's all right for me to practice here. The ceilings are so high that it seemed like the perfect place to work on my juggling without damaging anything."

"I don't see a problem with it." Faith didn't mention that she found it strange for him to be juggling right now.

But he seemed to know what she was thinking. "I've been searching everywhere for Gunther. You caught me taking a short break," he said sheepishly.

"How did Fiona take the news?" Faith asked.

"She's beside herself," Cody said. "To be honest, I need all the practice I can get with my juggling act because I may need to look for a new job after all this."

"Do you really think so?" Faith asked. "Does Fiona blame you for Gunther's disappearance?"

Cody fidgeted with the lapels of his suit and nodded. "I think she wants someone to blame, and I'm an easy target. Like I said before, Fiona has quite a temper. She doesn't always care who she directs it at."

"We can worry about Fiona later," Faith said. "Our first order of business is to find Gunther. The animal control officer is waiting in the conservatory, and he wants to ask you a few questions."

Cody crossed his muscular arms over his broad chest. "What good will that do? Gunther isn't in the conservatory."

"The officer thought there might be some kind of clue as to where he went," Faith answered. "Perhaps in your surprise at finding the terrarium empty, you overlooked a detail."

"I'm not a big fan of speaking with the authorities."

She wondered what could explain his reluctance. It wasn't as though he'd committed a crime by accidentally letting a snake loose. "Please come with me and talk to the animal control officer," she urged gently. "You might be able to help us locate Gunther."

Cody appeared uncertain for a moment, then dropped his arms to his sides. "Fine. Let's get it over with."

Faith and Cody were both silent as they walked to the conservatory.

She escorted the assistant inside and introduced him to Roland, who was studying a dense bed of greenery.

"I hope you can shed some light on things," Roland said to Cody. "Can you tell me about the last time you saw the python?"

"It was right over here," Cody said as he led the way to a spot pressed up against one of the long windows.

Nestled between a towering potted banana tree and a display of orchids in full bloom sat a large terrarium. It had been placed on one of the wheeled carts the staff used to transport supplies around the manor.

Faith approached the terrarium and peered inside. She tapped on the side of the glass and felt how sturdy the structure seemed. Although the lid was fashioned with only a metal mesh screen, there were no rips or holes in it. The screen had been weighed down securely with two lengths of pine boards and four pairs of red clay bricks. Clipped to one of the boards was a metal lamp with a flexible neck.

Cody pointed at the terrarium. "See? There's no way Gunther could have escaped."

"Are you sure that the bricks provided enough weight to keep the screen securely in place?" Faith asked. "Could he have pressed up on the mesh and created enough of a gap to slip through?"

"Of course I'm sure it was secure," Cody replied. "I've been taking care of Gunther for well over a year. I've never had him escape before, and I've used less weight than this to keep the lid on his terrarium. Plus, I recently installed a latch on the lid to make it even more foolproof."

"So you took extra precautions since you were away from home?" Roland asked.

"Exactly," Cody said. "I didn't want Gunther out loose where he might hurt himself, and I was concerned about the possibility of him bothering other guests."

"Obviously, there is no way that Gunther could have unlatched it," Roland said.

"But that would mean someone intentionally released him from the terrarium," Faith pointed out.

"Can you think of another explanation for his disappearance?" Roland asked, studying the terrarium from all sides.

Faith shivered as she glanced around the space. The leafy undergrowth and dappled patches of sunlight that had seemed so welcoming in the past now appeared menacing. Where better than the junglelike conditions of the conservatory for a snake to slither about?

Faith started inching toward the door. Then she stopped, telling herself to put her panic out of her mind and focus on the task at hand.

"Although this conservatory is the ideal spot for Gunther, he isn't in here now," Roland told them. "I'm going to search for him elsewhere in the building. Let me know if you find him." He strode out of the room.

Faith wondered who might have wanted to let the snake loose. "Is there any reason that someone might want to hurt Fiona by making her worry about her pet?"

She thought of Watson safely at home in her cottage. She knew how much her own animal companion meant to her, and she could well imagine that Fiona felt the same about Gunther. The loss of a pet would be devastating. It would take a cold person to do something like this deliberately.

"I can't think of anyone who'd wish her harm," Cody said. "Not to speak unkindly of my boss, but she's the one who is more likely to hold a grudge."

"Do you mean because of her injuries?" Faith asked.

Cody nodded. "She never got over being disfigured in the accident. The fact that she did not receive justice in the court system has only made her more bitter and angry over the years."

"Does she hold a grudge against anyone in particular?" Faith asked.

"Judge Davidson," Cody said.

"Why does she hold a grudge against him?"

"He was the one who ruled against her in her lawsuit," Cody explained.

Faith couldn't believe that the judge had presided over Fiona's lawsuit too. What were the odds? "Is there anyone else?"

"A little while ago, she was furious with the judge's nurse about her insistence that Gunther be kept hidden away. Fiona was fuming about it afterward."

Faith had overheard that argument. But Diana's main concern was keeping the snake away from the judge, and letting Gunther go would be counterproductive in that effort, as they would no longer know where he was, which meant the judge could encounter him anywhere. "Is that the sort of slight Fiona might take to heart?"

Cody shrugged. "I'm never quite sure what will set her off. Sometimes I think the accident didn't only disfigure her body but also her spirit. I like working for her most of the time, but she is notoriously short-tempered."

"I wonder if we should let the police know about the possibility that someone deliberately let Gunther out of the terrarium," Faith said.

"I'm not going to the police," Cody said vehemently. "If Fiona wants to let them know, then she can do it herself. Gunther is her property, not mine." Without another word or a backward glance, he stormed out of the room.

As Faith watched him go, a new thought occurred to her. Why was Cody so opposed to the idea of notifying the police?

Judging by the terrarium's security, it seemed most likely that someone had intentionally released Gunther. And now Faith had to wonder if that someone had been Cody.

But there was also Fiona. Could she have had a reason to let her own snake loose out of spite—or with some darker intent?

7

Faith felt more rattled by her conversation with Cody than she cared to admit. There was no way she was going to remain in the conservatory alone. With a final glance at the empty terrarium, she hurried out of the room.

As she walked down the hallway toward the library, she encountered Philip peering behind an antique silk screen from Japan. It was one of Faith's favorite decorative items in the manor's art collection, and she was pleased that someone else felt it deserved more than a passing glance.

"I see we share the same taste in collectibles," Faith said, pausing beside Philip.

"While I appreciate the craftsmanship, I was actually looking for the python," Philip admitted. "When Ms. Russell told me that the animal had disappeared, I offered to help with the search."

"That's exactly what I was about to do," Faith said. "Thanks for volunteering."

"Do you know how the snake got out in the first place?" Philip asked.

"No one is quite sure," Faith said. "His terrarium was secured and latched, so it's a bit of a mystery."

"Perhaps it's one of Fiona's magic tricks," Philip suggested.

While Faith had already suspected that Fiona might be responsible for the disappearance, she had not considered that it might be part of a magic act. Fiona certainly had a strong sense of the dramatic. But would she really do something so outrageous? Faith didn't know Fiona well enough to say for sure.

"According to Fiona's assistant, Cody, she is very upset about Gunther's disappearance," Faith said.

There was no reason for her to share her suspicions about either

Cody or Fiona with Philip. It was one thing to mention her worries about a snake on the loose. It was quite another to cast aspersions on the other guests.

"The manor is large, but he has to be here somewhere, right?" Philip asked. "So we'll have to be especially thorough. When Mr. Jaxon hired me, he mentioned the secret passages and hidden tunnels inside the manor. I wonder if Gunther could be hiding in one of them."

Faith had briefly considered that possibility, but she'd quickly shut down that train of thought. The idea of descending into the tunnels beneath the manor to look for an oversize python caused her pulse to race. Especially when she remembered the series of small rooms well beyond the wine cellar that reminded her of a castle's dungeon.

Philip seemed to realize that his words had upset her. "I could check out the tunnels for you."

Despite her overwhelming sense of relief, Faith felt guilty at his offer. "I couldn't ask you to do that."

"Nonsense. How often do you think I've gotten to see the sorts of nooks and crannies like the ones built into the manor?" Philip smiled. "In fact, you'd be doing me a big favor if you allowed me to search the tunnels. It would be fascinating."

"If you're absolutely sure, I'll let Ms. Russell know you're taking over that part of the building," Faith said. The tunnels, being underground, were much cooler than the upstairs, or even outside, so she thought it was unlikely Gunther was down there, since he was a heat-loving creature. Still, the tunnels did have to be checked out, and Philip seemed like the right person for the job.

"It's settled then," Philip said. "I'll let you know if I find anything. You'll do the same, won't you?"

"Absolutely."

After Philip walked away, she returned to the library to call Marlene.

"Do you have any news about the snake?" the assistant manager asked without preamble.

"The animal control officer is searching the building, and Philip Peters volunteered to check the tunnels," Faith reported.

"The staff is scouring the manor from top to bottom, and the groundskeepers and grooms are covering the outside of the property," Marlene said. "I need you to check in with the retreat guests at the log cabin. Laura will be there shortly to watch the library for you." Without waiting for a response, she hung up.

Laura Kettrick was always glad to step away from her usual housekeeping duties to assist Faith in the library. In fact, Laura was working her way through school to achieve her dream of becoming a librarian herself someday.

While Faith waited for Laura to arrive, she searched the library for any signs of the snake, then called Wolfe. She didn't know if Marlene had informed him about the situation yet, but she wanted to hear his voice. She sat down at her desk and took her cell phone from her pocket.

As soon as he answered, she felt a sense of comfort.

"I was just thinking of you," Wolfe said. "How are things at home?"

"I'm not sure you want to know," Faith said. "Do you remember that snake we met as you were leaving?"

"How could I forget Gunther?" he said with a chuckle. "What about him?"

"He's gone missing from his terrarium, and no one can find him." She filled him in on the search efforts.

"Well," Wolfe said when she finished, "it sounds like you and Marlene have everything as under control as it can be." His voice softened. "Is there anything I can do for you? I got the impression you weren't overly fond of huge snakes."

"Just talking to you is a real help," Faith admitted.

"I'll be home in a few days unless you need me to come back early."

Touched as she was by the offer, the last thing she wanted to do was interrupt his business trip. "I'm fine. Besides, I have Watson."

"Let me know if you need anything. I'll see you as soon as I can, Faith."

They said their goodbyes as Laura appeared in the doorway.

"Thanks for taking over the library for me," Faith said with a smile.

Laura approached Faith's desk. "I should thank you for getting me off snake patrol." The waifish young woman glanced around. "He's not in here, right?"

Faith shook her head. "Believe me, I've already searched every inch of the library. I've also kept the door closed, and I suggest you do the same. Guests can knock if they want to check out books."

"I will," Laura promised.

Faith collected the Laura Ingalls Wilder books she had promised to loan Pamela and slid them into a tote bag. With all the excitement over the lost snake, she hadn't had a chance to deliver them to her yet. She waved to Laura and headed off to the cabin.

It was with an unusual feeling of relief that she left the manor behind her and wandered through the garden on the way to the cabin. For some reason, she felt slightly safer outside.

The splendor of Castleton's gardens helped ease her mind as well. The manor's attentive gardeners expertly designed the grounds to showcase beauty in every season, even in the dead of winter.

But in May, Faith found the gardens particularly breathtaking. Lilacs and peonies were in various stages of budding and blooming. The very last of the narcissus bobbed cheerfully in the slight breeze. The roses were breaking into bud, and it would not be long before their heady scent filled the air.

Faith paused to view a gloriously blooming star magnolia. Its white blossoms were gorgeous during the day, but they were equally lovely to behold under the glow of moonlight.

Faith's cares and worries seemed to diminish with each step that she took toward the log cabin. By the time she arrived, her spirits were almost fully restored. Pamela's horse, Stormy, was hitched to a railing that ran around the cabin, and the covered wagon was parked on the other side. The scene was undeniably charming.

Faith mounted the steps and rapped on the cabin door.

Someone called for her to come in.

When Faith entered, she saw Terrence, Janine, Fiona, and the judge seated in rustic chairs in the living area of the cabin. The writers held notebooks and pens and seemed intent on improving their craft.

Diana was also present, but her attention was focused on Athena, who had wedged herself under the stove and was whining to be pried out.

Pamela sat in a chair at the front of the group, and she was again dressed in period costume. Today she wore a calico prairie skirt, a simple blouse, and vintage leather boots. She had braided her hair into two thick plaits.

Pamela crossed the room to meet Faith at the door. "I've just gotten the discussion back on track after all the hubbub about the snake," she said, her voice low. "If there isn't any news, I'd rather stay focused on the workshop."

"I don't have any updates, although Fiona would be the first to know if Gunther had been found. I certainly won't mention it for fear of upsetting her further." Faith handed the tote bag to Pamela. "Actually, I'm here to check in with you and deliver the Wilder materials you requested."

A look of relief spread over Pamela's face. "Oh, thank you. Would you care to join us?" she asked, motioning to an empty chair.

"I'd love to," Faith said, taking the seat.

Pamela returned to her seat and set the tote bag on her lap. "I've asked Miss Newberry to provide us with some inspiration for your own work. Laura Ingalls Wilder wrote down her tales in what we'd call creative nonfiction today. And in doing so, she left us an enduring legacy."

"She's one of my favorites," Janine commented. "And she's part of the reason why I'm here."

Faith was intrigued to see Fiona, Terrence, and even the judge nodding. She knew that Laura Ingalls Wilder appealed to young girls, but she had not realized the impact she had had on adults, even men.

"Obviously, she's one of my favorite authors too," Pamela said. "I'd like for us to use her example of mining someone's life for those details that make a story vivid and real."

"What do you mean by that?" the judge asked.

"Each one of you has a unique history and a compelling story to tell," Pamela responded. "But naturally there are commonalities from life to life and from well-told story to well-told story."

"It reminds me of my occupation. While all tricks and magicians are different, the same things make them successful," Fiona remarked from behind her veil. If she was upset about Gunther, she was hiding it well.

Faith's thoughts returned to her earlier suspicions. Had Fiona set her snake loose, perhaps to torment the judge because he ruled against her in her lawsuit?

"That's right," Pamela said. "For example, in the Little House on the Prairie series, Laura has an antagonist named Nellie Oleson."

"I remember her," Janine said. "Scenes with Nellie always made me keep turning pages."

"Me too," Pamela admitted. "Part of the reason the reader feels connected to Laura is because she shared both her triumphs and her tribulations."

"So including painful memories and unpleasant people or situations from our past will make our memoirs more interesting?" the judge asked.

Pamela nodded. "In fact, the more intense the emotion the author felt at the time, the more riveted the reader is likely to be. That is, as long as the author does a good job of conveying his or her feelings."

"It almost sounds like you're saying the story is better if there are more difficulties in it," Fiona said.

Faith wondered if Fiona was thinking of the loss of her pet or perhaps her own tragic accident. She had not seen the magician's injuries, but she was certain that Fiona wore a veil and long gloves to cover up scars marring her face, hands, and arms. Fiona probably had a very compelling story to tell.

"Protagonists with a great deal to overcome are the characters we find ourselves rooting for most, aren't they?" Pamela said. She pulled one of the books from the tote bag and held it up for the group to see.

Faith recognized the charming Garth Williams illustration on the cover of *The First Four Years*, the last book in the Little House on the Prairie series. To her mind, it was one of Wilder's most heartrending books. There had been so much hardship when Faith had really wanted an easy happily ever after for Laura. Of course, life was rarely like that.

"Were the difficulties that Laura faced along with her husband, Almanzo, in this book truly engrossing?" Pamela asked.

Everyone nodded.

Even Diana, who had finally managed to extricate Athena from beneath the stove, inched closer to the discussion and took a seat at the edge of the group.

"When patrons return books to the library, they rave about the ones where the protagonists struggle the most," Faith said. "The higher the mountain that needs climbing, the more satisfying readers find the summit."

"I couldn't have said it better myself." Pamela smiled at Faith, then addressed the writers in the group. "When you record times of extreme difficulty in your lives, make sure you convey your feelings and describe your antagonist, whether it was a person or a situation. If you keep these things in mind while you write, you will be well on your way to crafting scenes with real stakes and drama for your readers."

"I think that I speak for several people here who might say that the judge is the Nellie Oleson of their lives." Terrence leaned closer to the judge and punched him playfully on the upper arm, although his words had been anything but playful.

Pamela appeared taken aback at the hostility in Terrence's voice and at the turn the conversation had taken. Faith suddenly wondered if she knew about her students' previous connections. Judging by the shock on her face, Faith doubted it.

"Really, Mr. Hoyle, there is no need for that," Diana said. "The day has been quite upsetting enough without stirring things up even more."

Janine glanced at Faith and raised her eyebrows as if to ask whether Faith recalled the conversation they'd had in the library earlier. Then she stared down at the floor, shoulders hunched. The woman looked as though she would like to slip away through one of the cracks in the wide pine floor.

"There's no need to fuss," the judge told his nurse. "Mr. Hoyle is entitled to his own opinion. I assure you I think no better of him than he does of me."

The tips of Terrence's ears turned red, and the cocky smile he had worn while teasing the judge was quickly replaced by a scowl. He clenched and unclenched his fists, crumpling a few pages of his notebook without seeming to notice.

Faith felt as though she were seeing his real self for the first time, that dangerous side she'd sensed simmering under his joking demeanor.

"I doubt that very much," Terrence said through gritted teeth. "I'm sure it's far easier to look down your nose at me from the bench than it is to endure what I had to from you."

The judge chortled. "And what exactly did I do to you?"

"Do I have to remind you?" Terrence asked. "You cost me millions of dollars in attorneys' fees, damages, and stalled projects. You found against me every time my cases came before you!"

After feeling as if she'd escaped the manor only a short time ago, Faith now thought she might have had a more peaceful time back in the library, even if Gunther was curled up in one of the velvet chairs. She didn't like the coloring in Terrence's face, and she wondered if there was a possibility that he also suffered from some sort of cardiac problem or at least high blood pressure.

"I seem to recall that the last time you were in my courtroom I charged you only one dollar in damages," the judge retorted. "Surely a savvy businessman such as yourself was able to pay that with ease."

"Perhaps we should all try to forgive and forget while we're here for the retreat," Pamela said before another barb could be thrown. She sent a pleading look in Faith's direction.

Faith wasn't sure what she could do. Fiona and Janine were nodding ever so slightly at Terrence. Diana simply seemed puzzled. Perhaps she wasn't used to anyone contradicting her employer.

Terrence shot to his feet and glared at the judge. "I don't plan on forgiving, and I never forget. There is only one thing about me that you can be sure of. I'm planning to pay you back—with interest."

8

The next morning, Faith decided to leave Watson at the cottage again. Since Gunther was still on the loose, she didn't want to take any chances that her cat would run into the python somewhere inside the manor or on the grounds.

Before leaving, Faith gave Watson a tunaroon. "I'm sorry, but you can't go to the manor with me today. Stay here and be good."

The cat rubbed against her ankles as if reassuring her that he wouldn't get into trouble, then ate his treat with his usual delicacy.

As Faith made her way to the manor, she spotted Diana walking Athena.

Diana seemed lost in thought, and the little bulldog snuffled and shuffled through the shrubberies, pulling obstinately on her leash.

Faith wondered if she should speak to the nurse or leave her to her musings.

Athena suddenly barked at Faith.

Diana turned her head and gave Faith a faint smile. "You'll have to forgive Athena. She's still a bit agitated from the scene in the log cabin yesterday and the judge's mood this morning."

Athena tried to lunge at Faith's ankles, but Diana held the dog back.

"She doesn't seem to like me very much," Faith remarked, wondering if the stray strands of Watson's fur that were undoubtedly clinging to her pant legs contributed to Athena's apparent dislike of her.

"It isn't you," Diana said. "I think she's also out of sorts because I'm the one walking her again instead of the judge."

"How is he?" Faith asked. She wasn't sure whether she was asking after the judge's health or his attitude after the outburst in yesterday's workshop. He'd seemed almost gleeful when he needled Terrence about the unfavorable decisions he'd handed down.

A slight crackling sound, like the breaking of a branch, caught her attention.

Athena seemed to hear it too. She pricked her ears and strained against her leash toward the dense bushes.

Faith couldn't shake the feeling there was someone or something hidden out of sight, watching them. She shuddered. Was it Gunther?

"I almost think the judge enjoyed hearing what Mr. Hoyle had to say," Diana responded. She started walking again. "It was as if he was able to relive times gone by."

"Do you think he misses his time on the bench?" Faith glanced behind her, but no person—or animal—followed them.

"I believe that's a big reason he wants to write his memoirs," Diana said.

"You sound as though you don't entirely approve."

"Not necessarily," Diana replied. "But I can't help but wonder if the judge may be opening a can of worms by writing about his life."

"He wouldn't be the first powerful person to write a tell-all in his senior years," Faith pointed out.

"No, but I also worry that it's going to be hard on his health to be here this week." Diana tugged Athena away from a large holly bush. "He tends to enjoy more conflict than is good for him."

"I confess, I overheard your conversation with Fiona and Cody concerning the snake," Faith said. "Fiona didn't sound like she would be content to let bygones be bygones either."

"That's exactly the sort of thing I mean. There are real risks for a man in his condition, even when he isn't faced with unusual levels of stress."

Faith thought back to the tone of Fiona's voice as she had dismissed Diana's pleas for her to move her snake out of the conservatory. If the judge needed a low-stress environment to preserve his health, Faith had an uncomfortable feeling he had picked the wrong week to visit Castleton Manor—and the wrong writers group as well.

"Do you think the confrontational atmosphere will prove to be too much for him?" Faith asked.

"I am worried about that, but I have another concern too." Diana bent down and removed a leaf from Athena's smooth coat. "What worries me most is that Mr. Hoyle might not have been exaggerating when he said he was planning to pay the judge back."

"Maybe he was simply speaking in the heat of the moment," Faith suggested. "Some people lose their tempers quite easily."

"That's just it, though, isn't it?" Diana said. "This retreat isn't about things that are happening in the moment. It's about remembering, even reliving the past."

Faith knew what Diana was getting at. When Terrence had voiced his harsh comments, he'd seemed as if his anger and frustration had simmered and stewed over time until they reached a boiling point.

"I wonder if too much is getting stirred up," Diana continued. "Pamela even seems to be encouraging her students to dredge up the worst parts of their lives."

"She must be trying to help them get the most out of the retreat," Faith said soothingly, although she wondered the same thing.

Diana was silent as she stared off into the distance.

Faith followed her gaze but saw nothing more interesting than a gray squirrel scampering across the velvety green lawn.

"You're probably right. I'm sure I'm worrying for no reason," Diana finally said.

"I hope you'll be able to set aside the unpleasantness and enjoy your time at the manor," Faith told her.

"I'll certainly try. It is a wonderful place." Diana let Athena's leash out, and the dog took the opportunity to snuffle around in a wider circle. "Pamela's workshop did make me wonder something."

"What's that?"

"Whether I should sit down and write my own memoir one day."

"You must have had a lot of interesting cases during the course of your career," Faith said.

Diana nodded. "I worked at several hospitals in the Boston area over the years, and some of the stories I could tell would give you goose bumps."

"I can only imagine," Faith said. "You must have seen many life-and-death situations."

"That is true." Diana paused. "Did you know I was on duty the night the ambulance brought Fiona in after her accident?"

Faith started but quickly recovered. "Did you assist with her emergency care?"

"No," Diana said. "I was in cardiology that night. That has been my specialty for most of my career. But I heard a great deal about it from the other members of the staff."

"I'm sure having a celebrity in the hospital was very chaotic and difficult to deal with," Faith commented.

"The media made it hard for anyone to get in and out of the hospital," Diana said. "And the gossip that flew around for weeks was like nothing I had ever seen before."

"It was a dramatic situation," Faith stated.

She remembered that the tragedy had been on the front page of the papers for almost a week until a sudden autumn blizzard buried the area in three feet of snow. Even after that, Fiona's accident and her recovery had been written about for a few more weeks, especially on slow news days. When Fiona had announced her intention to mount a case against the company that had built her props for the show, the media frenzy had started up all over again.

"I should say so. The papers and television reporters were relentless. I followed every little bit of it at the time." Diana shook her head. "I never thought I would end up working for someone who had been involved in the case."

"Have you ever discussed it with the judge?" Faith asked, her curiosity getting the better of her.

"I make it my business to upset my patients as little as possible." Diana gave Athena a gentle tug on the leash.

The bulldog trotted over to her side.

"So you think he would be upset by talking about her case?" Faith asked. "I can't imagine he would want to leave that one out of his memoir."

"I'm sure he wouldn't," Diana replied. "It was one of the most famous cases he ever presided over."

"It surprised me that Fiona didn't win," Faith said. "The newspapers predicted that she would."

"I know. The poor woman suffered so much. It seemed downright cruel when the court case went against her."

"Perhaps she'll write about it in her memoir," Faith suggested, recalling how Fiona had hinted as much when she first arrived.

"I'll buy a copy if she ever has it published, but I'll have to hide the book from my employer," Diana said, then gestured to Athena. "We're going to take another turn around the garden before we go in. Would you like to join us?"

Faith shook her head. "I wish I could, but I need to get to the library."

"Sure thing. We'll see you later." Diana waved as she strode away. Athena waddled next to her at a good clip.

She had to agree with Diana that there was ill will brewing among the guests. That on top of an absent python made Faith feel apprehensive.

Speaking of the python, she had to investigate the noise she'd heard. She found a stick, steeled herself, and lifted the lower branches of the large holly bush, then peered under it from as far away as the stick would allow.

She gave a sigh of relief as she realized there was no ten-foot snake coiled around the trunk. There were only branches and shiny green leaves.

Still, a shiver ran up her spine, and she couldn't shake the feeling that someone—or something—had been hiding there, watching and listening to their entire conversation.

Despite having left Watson locked inside her cottage, Faith was dismayed, though not surprised, to find him stationed near the doorway when she arrived at the library. The cat had a way of turning up in the most unexpected places, and she had never quite figured out how he got around.

She unlocked the door, and Watson disappeared inside the library.

In case Gunther had some of the same skills Watson did, Faith carefully scanned the spaces under each piece of furniture as she went to her desk.

After assuring herself that the coast was clear, she sat down and tried to focus on preparing a to-do list. She pulled one of her favorite pens from the ornate holder on her desk and opened a notebook, then jotted down the day's tasks in order of importance.

She needed to check with Marlene to see if there was any news about Gunther. But first she would catalog new materials. That would take only a few minutes, and it would be nice to have that out of the way before she spoke to Marlene, in case the assistant manager accused her of neglecting her duties.

Faith entered the information into her computer, then shelved the books and crossed off the task when she returned to her desk and sat down again.

Watson jumped onto her lap, startling her.

She heard a noise at the door and turned.

Judge Davidson stood in the doorway, his arms folded over his chest with the sort of look Faith always associated with a bad case of indigestion.

She gently urged Watson down from her lap and rose in greeting. "Welcome to the library, Judge Davidson. I'm glad you stopped by."

The judge snorted loudly as he walked over to her. "Really?"

"I'm always happy to show a guest around our library," Faith replied. Watson rubbed against her leg.

The judge scowled down at the cat. "I've always been far too busy for pleasure reading. I certainly don't intend to start now."

Faith couldn't imagine a life without the joy of reading, but here was living proof that such people existed. She had to wonder why someone with no desire to read would be interested in writing a book himself.

"Fiction, magazines, and all that sort of tripe is simply not worth my time," the judge continued. "But I do make a point to keep up with articles in quality newspapers, and I occasionally read military history."

"Do you enjoy biographies or memoirs of well-known figures?" Faith asked.

His expression told her that his answer should be obvious. "I've spent my entire career listening to other people's sob stories and versions of events. I refuse to spend my retirement years similarly engaged."

Faith had not considered that the courtroom was a kind of stage for an unceasing number of personal dramas to unfold, but it made sense. From personal injury to financial disaster, there was enough fodder for many, many volumes, as evidenced by the judge's fellow memoirists.

"So what brings you here? I believe all the writers, not just your group, are meeting up later this morning for a lecture by Pamela." Faith checked her watch. "You still have some time before that. Perhaps you'd like to sit down and take in the ocean view while you wait," she suggested, indicating a velvet seat near the French doors.

"I thought this might be where I would find Nurse Marsden," the judge said, scanning the room. "The silly woman always has her nose stuck in a book whenever she thinks I'm not paying attention."

"She hasn't been in yet," Faith responded.

"Where can she have gotten to?" the judge growled.

"I spoke to her not long ago," Faith said. "She was outside walking Athena. The last I knew, she was planning to come back in soon, so I imagine she's around here somewhere."

The judge rubbed a fist into his sternum. "Diana has always been such a reliable employee, except for all the reading she does. If she's off doing that now instead of doing what I pay her for—" He broke off and collapsed into a nearby chair.

Faith rushed over to him. "Do you need her for a medical reason?"

"Of course I need her for a medical reason," the judge barked. His face started to turn purple, and his breath came in labored gasps. "Why else would I spend money for a private nurse?"

Before Faith could decide what to do—call 911 or race to find Diana—Marlene stepped into the library.

The judge made a strangled noise and clutched at his chest. Then he toppled out of the chair, landing on the floor in a heap.

Marlene hurried over to the judge. She whipped out her cell phone and called 911, judging from her side of the conversation.

Faith bent over him to see if he was still breathing. "Judge Davidson?"

His eyes fluttered open, and he stared at her with an unfocused gaze.

She reached for the judge's wrist and felt for his pulse. It was faint and erratic.

As Marlene talked to the dispatcher, the assistant manager removed her jacket, folded it into a neat rectangle, and slid it under the judge's head.

"Angina. I need my pills," the judge said in a feeble voice.

"Where are they?" Faith asked.

"By the bed in my room," he said, barely above a whisper.

"I'll stay here with him and wait for the paramedics." Marlene handed Faith her master key. "You fetch his pills. He's in the Arthur Conan Doyle Suite."

Faith ran all the way to the judge's room on the second floor, taking the stairs two at a time with Watson close on her heels. Her hand trembled slightly as she unlocked the door, and she took a deep breath before entering.

A barrage of barks assaulted her. Athena must be here, although the heavy drapes were still drawn and the room was bathed in shadows, so she couldn't see the dog. Faith fumbled for the light switch next to the door and flicked it on.

Watson dashed away from her side to explore the room.

Out of the corner of her eye, she saw the tip of his bobbed tail disappear around the edge of a richly upholstered wingback chair.

Athena sat inside a kennel on a small plaid dog bed with her name embroidered on the front, right next to the fireplace that anchored one side of the room. She lurched to her feet and growled when she spotted Watson.

A king-size bed covered in a sumptuous velvet duvet and a profusion of pillows was positioned against the far wall. On each side of the bed stood a carved mahogany nightstand. Faith could see a pill bottle on the right-hand nightstand.

As she started to cross the room to fetch it, Watson yowled. She tried to ignore him because the judge desperately needed his medicine.

Athena continued to growl.

Faith took another step toward the bedside table, but Watson became louder and more insistent from the corner of the room. With reluctance, she changed course and raced around the side of the cozy reading chair.

There, sprawled on the floor in front of a floor-to-ceiling bookcase, lay the motionless body of Diana.

9

Faith gasped and rushed to the nurse's side. With a feeling of déjà vu, she dropped to her knees and felt Diana's wrist for a pulse.

Unlike the judge, there was none to be found.

Diana wasn't old and hadn't seemed unhealthy, so it seemed unlikely that she had suddenly collapsed from a heart attack.

Faith wondered if she simply wasn't skilled enough to feel for a pulse at the wrist. She loosened Diana's collar and placed her fingers along her neck.

She held her breath as she studied Diana's face. She desperately hoped to feel even the faintest flicker of a pulse or see the barest flutter of her eyes.

After a long moment, she had to give up. It was clear that Diana would never walk Athena or read another book again.

As she drew her hand away, something about the nurse's neck caught Faith's attention. She leaned in to take a closer look. There was a wide discolored mark all along her throat. Was it a bruise that hadn't fully developed yet? Unless she missed her guess, Diana's death had involved foul play. But who would do such a thing?

Faith knew better than to further disturb the body any more than she'd already done, so she resisted the urge to lift Diana's head to check if the marks ran all the way around the back of her neck.

However, she had already lost too much time on this. It was obvious there was nothing more she could do for Diana, and she needed to take the judge his pills.

Faith snatched the bottle from the nightstand and slipped it into her pocket. Then she found Athena's leash hanging over the back of a chair and opened the kennel. After some cajoling, she was able to get the dog out. She clipped the leash on Athena's collar and led her to the door.

Watson raced out into the hallway in front of them.

Faith locked the door behind her and raced toward the library.

She wished she could stay with Diana. It seemed so unkind to leave her alone in the suite, but there was nothing else to do. If she didn't get the medicine to the judge promptly, there might be another tragedy. And what if the judge took a turn for the worse when he found out about his nurse?

Suddenly, another upsetting thought occurred to her, and she stopped dead in her tracks.

Athena pulled up short with a grunt of annoyance.

"Sorry," she said, and they rushed forward again as Faith continued to think.

The mark around Diana's neck had been quite wide, and Faith's first thought upon seeing it had been that she had been strangled. But now she realized it seemed too wide and too uniform to have been made by bare human hands.

Faith cast her mind back to the scene around the body. There had been nothing near it that could have been used for that horrible purpose—unless it was hidden inside the room somewhere.

Of course it was likely that if someone had killed Diana, he or she had brought the murder weapon and then had taken it away again after the deed was done.

But there was another possibility that Faith found equally chilling. What if Diana hadn't been murdered at all? What if she had been going about her business in the judge's suite and somehow the python had slipped inside and killed her?

Faith broke into a sprint, Athena struggling to keep up with her.

When they burst into the library, Faith rushed over to Marlene with Athena huffing next to her.

Watson apparently didn't want to be around when Faith broke

the news. He retreated to one of the chairs in front of the fireplace.

Marlene frowned. "I'll be sure to ask anyone else on staff to fetch my pills if I'm ever in a situation like this myself. Need I remind you that we have a medical emergency here?"

Faith raised her finger to her lips and motioned toward the judge. His eyes were closed, but he might still be conscious. She was not going to discuss Diana in front of him, at least not until he had been seen by a medical professional and had been deemed fit to hear such news.

Marlene was wise enough to understand that something else had happened. Instead of asking any more questions, she held out her hand.

Faith passed her the bottle of pills, and Marlene read the label.

Before she could twist off the cap, the judge's eyes snapped open, and he snatched the bottle from her hand. He popped off the lid and shook a tablet under his tongue, then collapsed back and closed his eyes once more.

The wail of an ambulance siren sounded. Help was almost here.

Soon three EMTs arrived in the library and expertly took over care of the judge.

As they bustled around him with various pieces of medical equipment, Faith heaved a sigh of relief. She and Marlene were no longer responsible for his health.

Marlene motioned for Faith to follow her to the far side of the library where they would not be overheard by the judge or the paramedics. "What in the world took you so long?" Marlene demanded. "Weren't his pills where he said they would be?"

"I found them right on his bedside table, but there's something else." Faith swallowed. "I wasn't looking for Diana, but I did find her."

"What a relief. I can call off that search." Marlene cocked her head. "Why didn't you bring her down here with you?"

"She's dead," Faith whispered. She had not planned to be so abrupt in breaking the news, but at least she somehow managed to keep her voice low.

Marlene's jaw dropped open, and her eyes widened. "Dead? How can that be?"

"I don't know," Faith said. "I found her on the floor in Judge Davidson's suite."

"Did you check for a pulse?" Marlene asked.

"I checked for one at her wrist and then at her neck," Faith said. "There were marks around her throat—as though she had been strangled by something smooth and wide."

Marlene reached for her own throat in a protective gesture. "Do you think she was murdered?"

"I'm not sure," Faith admitted.

"I thought you said she was strangled," Marlene said. "Do you think she got tangled up by her own scarf or something?"

Faith shook her head. "Nothing like that. In fact, I didn't see anything that could have been used to strangle her."

"You aren't making any sense. If she was strangled and it wasn't an accident, then how can she not have been murdered?" Marlene put her hands on her hips as she waited for an answer.

"The width of the mark around her neck made me wonder if it was possible that Fiona's python somehow slipped into the judge's suite and caught Diana by surprise."

"What?" Marlene's gaze darted around the library. "You think the missing snake may have killed her?"

A shiver ran up Faith's back. "I don't know, but the thought did cross my mind."

"I'll talk to the paramedics and explain the situation." Marlene crossed the room and pulled one of the EMTs aside.

The paramedic nodded and said something to her partner, then followed Marlene out of the room.

The judge seemed to have made a strong recovery after receiving his medication. After a few minutes, he was able to sit up and converse with the EMTs.

Faith unclipped Athena's leash, and the dog bounded over to her master and plunked down next to him.

"We're going to take you to the hospital now," the paramedic said.

"I'm not going to the hospital," the judge said irritably. "All I want is to go back to my suite and lie down." He scanned the room. "Where's my nurse?"

Faith glanced at the door and noticed Marlene and the other EMT standing in the doorway.

Marlene shook her head at Faith as if to say Diana was officially beyond hope, then nodded toward the judge.

It would fall to Faith to tell him what had happened. At least there were emergency personnel here in case the news gave him more of a shock than his weakened heart could handle.

She took a deep breath and approached the judge. "I'm so sorry to tell you this, but there has been an incident involving Diana. I'm afraid she has passed away."

Judge Davidson gaped at her. "How?"

"I'm really not sure," Faith said.

"But that is preposterous," he said. "She was never ill. Never."

Marlene joined them. "I really think you should go to the hospital and at least stay overnight," she told the judge. "We don't have medical personnel on staff in case you have another incident."

The judge huffed. "Nonsense. I'm not going to miss out on the retreat because of a little angina."

What a cold, dreadful man, Faith thought. His private nurse was dead, and all he seemed concerned about was the retreat.

"The shock of your nurse's death probably hasn't sunk in quite yet," Marlene said, putting on her professional demeanor, even though she was probably every bit as disconcerted as Faith by the judge's apparent apathy.

"I am hardly going to work myself up over the demise of an employee," he said, getting to his feet.

Out of the corner of her eye, Faith noticed Watson's ears flatten against his head as if he could not believe what he'd just heard. She had to agree with her cat's assessment. The judge was completely self-centered and callous.

"I want to lie down in my room immediately," the judge said in a tone that brooked no argument.

Marlene turned to the paramedics. "Is it all right if he stays here?"

"He seems to have made a good recovery," one of the EMTs said. "He shows no lingering signs of distress, and his vitals are strong. If he doesn't wish to seek additional medical attention, we can't force him."

Marlene nodded, then addressed the judge. "The police need to cordon off your suite for the time being. If you refuse to be checked out at the hospital, I will have to move you to a different room."

The judge waved his hand dismissively. "Fine. Let's go. And bring my dog."

Marlene picked up Athena's leash and clipped it back on the dog's collar. "Right this way, sir."

Faith was glad that Marlene was in charge of that particular task. Judge Davidson was not an easy man to deal with.

10

Faith returned the library to its former order, including the furniture that had been displaced by the judge and the paramedics.

A little later, Marlene strode into the room. "I've moved Judge Davidson to the Charles Dickens Suite."

"How is he doing?" Faith asked.

"He seems to be all right, but I wish he would have gone to the hospital."

"Any news about the snake?"

Marlene shook her head. "Since the animal control officer failed to locate the animal, I've called in every available staff member to search the premises."

"I hope someone finds Gunther soon," Faith remarked.

"I do too." Marlene checked her watch. "I'd better go. I need to check in with Chief Garris. He's going over the Doyle suite." She swept out of the room.

Faith sat down at her desk, filled with a nervous energy that made simply following her to-do list impossible. She sent a text to Wolfe to tell him what was going on. She assured him she was fine and she'd be in touch again the moment there was more information.

Then she answered a few e-mails, but the activity didn't help take her mind off what she had witnessed. She continued to see Diana's lifeless body sprawled on the floor in the judge's suite. No matter how many times she told herself that Gunther couldn't possibly be here in this room, she couldn't stop scanning the library for signs of his presence.

It was with deep relief that Faith greeted Chief Andy Garris when he entered the library a little later. Faith had come to see the chief as a reliable and welcome presence anytime something distressing occurred at the manor. She had always found him to be fair, kind, and intelligent.

"Ms. Russell told me that you're the one who found Ms. Marsden's body," Garris said, his tone sympathetic.

"Yes," she said simply.

"Why don't we take a seat, and then you can tell me all about it?" the chief said. "As long as you feel up to it, that is."

Faith nodded and led him to the chairs facing the huge fireplace. Watson was still curled up in one of them. She took a seat next to her cat, and Garris sat down in the chair on the other side of her.

Somehow simply sitting here helped her feel much calmer. But that was just like the chief. He knew how to bring out the best in witnesses and suspects alike and seemed to do so effortlessly.

Garris pulled a notepad and a pen from his pocket. He opened the notepad and propped it on his knee, then turned to her. "I understand the judge collapsed here in the library, and you went up to his suite to retrieve his medication. Is that correct?"

Faith let out a sigh. "Yes, that's right. Although everything happened so fast that it seems like a blur."

"Take your time and tell me exactly what you remember. Everything you saw and heard."

"I left the judge in the library with Marlene and ran upstairs to get his pills," Faith said. "I used Marlene's master key to unlock the door. When I entered the room, Watson went in with me. He immediately let me know there was something wrong, and when I followed him to see what it was, I discovered Diana on the floor."

The chief jotted down notes. "Are you certain Ms. Marsden was already dead when you found her?"

Faith frowned. "I hoped that she wasn't, so I checked for a pulse in her wrist, then her neck. By the time I left her to take the judge his pills, I was sure there was no hope of saving her."

"And you saw no sign of a weapon or anything to indicate

who might have been in the suite with her?" Garris asked, leaning forward slightly.

"Nothing at all," Faith replied. "I wondered if she'd had a heart attack since I didn't notice any signs of a struggle or any sort of violence."

"But something made you change your mind about that?" the chief said.

"That's right. When I checked her throat for a pulse, I noticed the broad mark around her neck." Faith gulped. "She was strangled, wasn't she?"

"I can't say for certain until the medical examiner has had a chance to view the body," he explained. "However, it appears to me that the cause of death was most likely strangulation."

"I was afraid you were going to say that," Faith responded.

"Do you have any idea why anyone might want to harm her?" Garris continued.

Faith was startled by the question. She hadn't considered any specific suspects other than Gunther, let alone any possible motives. After all, what motive could a snake have had?

"I have no idea who would have wanted to harm Diana," Faith admitted. "For the most part, she seemed to be a pleasant woman."

"But even pleasant people can make enemies," the chief pointed out.

He was right. She thought back to the interactions Diana had had with the other guests since arriving at the manor. "From what I saw, she didn't talk to many people other than the judge. But she did argue with Fiona Perkins and her assistant, Cody James, quite heatedly."

"Do you know what they were arguing about?"

"The judge has a terrible phobia of snakes, and Diana was upset that Fiona had placed her python's terrarium in the conservatory where the judge might come across it unexpectedly."

"Do you think Ms. Perkins and Mr. James would have taken sufficient offense to lash out and murder her over something like that?" the chief said.

"Fiona seemed really offended by the nurse's concerns," Faith said.

"Offended enough to kill someone?" Garris persisted.

"I don't believe so. Not unless there was something more behind it. It was only an argument."

"Is there anything else you can think of?" he asked.

"There was a bit of a dustup at a gathering of one of the writers groups yesterday," Faith told him.

"What kind of dustup?" Garris asked.

"Terrence Hoyle accused the judge of ruling against him and costing him millions of dollars," Faith explained. "Diana came to the judge's defense, and Terrence didn't seem too pleased about it."

The chief tapped his pen on the notepad. "Terrence Hoyle. Why does that name sound familiar?"

"He admitted that he's been in court more than once," Faith said. "Perhaps you heard about his cases."

"Yes, that's probably it. I'll take a closer look at him. Although why he would target Ms. Marsden rather than the judge is a mystery."

Faith suddenly thought of something else. "There was one other thing about Diana."

"What was that?" he said.

"I came across her walking the judge's dog earlier and paused to speak with her for a few moments. While we were talking, I could have sworn someone was hiding in the bushes and listening to our conversation."

Garris studied her. "Are you sure? You don't think you might have imagined it?"

"I considered that at first," Faith said. "It's easy to let your imagination run away with you, and that's awfully cloak-and-dagger. But the judge's dog, Athena, seemed to notice something too. She tried to duck under the bushes when I thought I heard rustling on the other side."

"It might have been a squirrel or a chipmunk," the chief suggested.

"That's true, but I couldn't shake the feeling we were being observed."

"Thank you for telling me about that. Your instincts are often spot-on, and I appreciate your input. Is there anything else?"

"Diana mentioned that attending this session of the writers group with the judge had given her the idea to consider writing her own memoirs," Faith said, recalling the rest of the conversation. "She told me she'd had quite a lot of interesting cases over the years. I wonder if she might have known something one of the guests would not like to have written down."

The chief took some more notes. "That's an interesting possibility as well. I'll track down Ms. Marsden's former employers and see if there might be anything to it."

"If it helps, she said she worked at a number of hospitals in the Boston area," Faith said.

"Thanks. That will give me somewhere to start."

"There's one last thing," Faith said. "Have you heard about Gunther?"

Garris slid his notepad and pen into his pocket. "Is he a guest here at the manor?"

"He's one of our animal guests. He's Fiona's pet python."

"And how does a snake come into this?" the chief asked.

"Unfortunately, Gunther is . . . Well, we don't know where he is. The staff and Roland from animal control have been diligently searching for him, but he hasn't been found. He's roaming about freely somewhere inside the manor, or he may have made it out onto the grounds by now."

Garris frowned. "You think a snake may have done this to the nurse?"

"The thought did cross my mind," Faith said. "Roland told me that it is not unknown for pythons to injure or even kill humans."

The chief must have detected something in her expression because he reached out and gently placed a hand on her shoulder. "I'll talk to Roland about it, but he has a reputation for knowing his job. If he hasn't already asked you to clear the premises, I don't believe there's much risk to anyone."

"But someone is responsible for what happened to Diana," Faith said. "Even if Gunther didn't harm her, someone did."

Garris nodded. "Until the guilty party is found, I can't in good conscience promise that anyone is entirely safe, whether the snake in the grass is literal or figurative."

Faith shuddered. Even after Gunther was caught and Diana's killer was found, it might be a very long time before she felt safe again.

"I've already told the guests to remain on the premises," he said. "I'll be questioning them soon."

When the chief left the room, Faith got up and went over to her desk. She sat down and took out her to-do list, but she didn't take in any of the words on it. Her mind kept returning to Diana's murder.

She jumped when Watson rubbed against her ankles. She bent down and lifted him into her lap.

He kneaded her legs with his soft paws and turned around several times before curling into a ball, purring.

She frowned at her to-do list, then grabbed her phone and texted Wolfe a summary of her conversation with the chief.

Faith wished she could call Midge for her expert veterinary advice. Faith knew that Midge would have some insight into a python's preferred hiding places. No one else was as knowledgeable about animals' habits as Midge—probably not even Roland, though she appreciated his continued search efforts at the manor.

Unfortunately, Midge would not be back until later in the week, and Faith had no intention of worrying her friend while she was away on her well-deserved trip with her husband, Peter.

Besides, her conversation with the chief had made her wonder if Diana's death was the work of one of the manor's human guests. But if so, who?

Faith ran the suspects through her mind—Fiona, Cody, and Terrence. She had mentioned the quarrels Diana had had with other guests to the chief, but she still found it hard to believe that any of those arguments would lead someone to murder.

She needed to come at this from a different angle. She had seen Diana walking Athena only that morning, so presumably Diana had been in the judge's room to return the dog. Maybe Diana had let one of the other guests in while she was there alone. But surely the nurse would not have done so if the person had appeared threatening in any way. Perhaps someone knew the judge was downstairs and followed her to the suite, sneaking in behind her when she'd opened the door.

Judge Davidson had been searching for Diana, but she had been in his room. How had he not known where she was? Diana must have arrived at the suite shortly after he searched for her there—if he did at all. Yet from what Faith had seen, Diana had been extremely attentive to her patient, so it was surprising that the judge had not known where to find her or how to contact her.

And what about Athena? Had the dog barked and growled from her kennel when someone entered the room?

Faith couldn't be sure if Athena had felt any loyalty to Diana or not. Every time she had seen the two of them together, the dog seemed intent on pursuing her own interests—like snuffling under bushes or barking at cats.

Diana had not appeared too pleased with her responsibilities for the dog either. Faith supposed it was possible that Athena would not have put up much of a fuss if someone had meant Diana harm. Had the nurse carried out dog-walking duties during her entire tenure as the judge's nurse, or was it a new responsibility since his surgery?

The walls in the suites were thick and made of sound-muffling plaster and paneling. With the heavy drapes, plush carpeting, and thick wooden doors in each of the rooms, Faith knew most guests happily reported that they had never experienced a more peaceful night's sleep at a hotel.

Therefore, there was the possibility that Athena could have sounded quite an alarm but no one had heard her, especially since the guests likely had been going for breakfast or heading to workshops on the main floor. Still, someone in the rooms nearby or passing along the corridor might have heard barking or other noises coming from the judge's suite.

She assumed Chief Garris had already questioned the guests or was planning to, but she thought it might be worth following up on.

There was a fairly small window when the death could have happened. Faith had talked to Diana not an hour before the judge came into the library searching for her.

Faith decided she would make discreet inquiries of the other guests. She owed that much to Diana, considering she might have been the last person—other than the killer—to see her alive.

Another thought occurred to Faith. The python might not only be hiding somewhere, but he could be injured somehow. Faith was surprised to find that she was actually worried about the snake's welfare. If Gunther had attacked Diana, he was only being true to his nature and couldn't be blamed the way a human could.

But even so, the snake was undeniably dangerous. Gunther had to be found—and the sooner the better.

11

As Faith headed back to the library after delivering a book to a guest, she overheard the sound of angry voices. She paused, then crept quietly toward the noise.

While she didn't usually make it a habit to eavesdrop on the guests, her concerns about the activities at the manor pushed her scruples to the back burner.

She recognized the voices of Cody and Judge Davidson.

"I have a bone to pick with you, young man," the judge said.

"I can't imagine why," Cody said. His words were defiant, but Faith thought she caught a slight tone of fear.

"I've been asking around, and you're the last person to have seen that snake. If I have another angina attack, I'll hold you personally responsible."

"Your nurse made it abundantly clear when we first arrived that you weren't a big fan of Gunther," Cody responded. "But I can't see how your phobia and your bad health are my fault."

Faith peeked around the corner. The two men were facing each other in the hallway, and they both appeared angry. The judge waved his hand in Cody's face. Cody stood with his legs set in a wide stance and his arms folded across his chest.

"I'm warning you," the judge said. "If I find out you had anything to do with that snake getting loose, you'll regret it."

Cody laughed. "What are you going to do, old man?"

"I remember who you are."

"What's that supposed to mean?" Cody said. Now the fear in his voice was unmistakable.

She peeked around the corner again and saw that Cody had taken a step back from the judge.

"Even though it has been some time since you appeared in my courtroom, I haven't forgotten about your criminal record," the judge said. "I never forget a defendant's face."

"That's all behind me now. I did my time. I've turned over a new leaf."

"You're not the first hoodlum to stand before me and make such a claim," the judge huffed.

"I've got a good job, and I've been working at it for over a year," Cody said. "What do you have against me?"

"You're a convicted criminal and a person who handles snakes," the judge replied. "I hate them both. If you're responsible for this, I'm going to make certain the parole board hears about it."

"Are you sure you want to make that kind of threat?" Cody said, his voice taking on a steely edge.

"I'm not making a threat. I'm stating a fact. You'll end up serving the remainder of your sentence behind bars rather than flitting about on Fiona's arm. I'm the one in a position of power here."

Faith peered around the corner once more. As much as she didn't want to be discovered eavesdropping, she needed to see the judge's reaction and the look on Cody's face.

"You may think that you're the one in control of this situation, but all I see is a frail old man with a heart condition," Cody said evenly. "If you'd like to have a future, you'd better stop talking about my past." The magician's assistant turned his back on the judge and marched straight for the end of the hall where Faith stood. Gone was the pleasant young man with the bright smile.

Faith considered what sort of crime Cody had committed. Then she realized that poor Diana's name hadn't even been mentioned—the judge had only seemed concerned about the snake. But from the look of pure hatred on Cody's face, she couldn't help but wonder if she'd been staring at a killer.

Although she thought twice about confronting Cody when he appeared so angry, Faith reached out her hand and stopped him in his tracks. "Are you okay? It sounds like there's no love lost between you and Judge Davidson."

"You heard that?" he said, deflating before her very eyes.

"I'm afraid I did."

"You're probably wondering why I was arrested."

"It isn't any of my business," Faith said, although she certainly wanted to know in order to reassure herself that this young man wasn't dangerous. "But I have been known to be a good listener if you want to talk about it."

Cody studied her for a moment and then let out a sigh. "Right after I turned eighteen, I stole a car. I had fallen in with a bad crowd and made some choices I regret." He met her eyes, and there was only sadness in them. "I did my time, and I thought I had put the past behind me."

"Does Fiona know about your record?" Faith asked.

"I told her during my initial interview, and she gave me the chance to start over. I've done nothing wrong ever since my release, so it really bothers me that the judge is threatening to have my parole revoked for something I didn't do."

"If you haven't done anything wrong, then you have no reason to worry," Faith said soothingly. "You don't think the judge will be able to convince Fiona to fire you, do you?"

"Like I've said before, Fiona has an unpredictable temper. Who knows what she's capable of doing? But I think if she was going to fire me for losing Gunther, she would have done it by now."

Faith recalled Diana's confrontation with Fiona. Perhaps it would have seemed like a small matter to anyone else, but could it have enraged Fiona enough that she was willing to kill over it? Maybe there had been another argument between Fiona and Diana that no one else had overheard. Perhaps it had turned violent and Fiona had lashed out.

"Your suite and Fiona's are both near Judge Davidson's, aren't they?" Faith asked, trying to gauge his reaction. If he'd been questioned by the chief about Diana's death, he gave no sign.

"Yes. We're right across the hallway," Cody said, a note of caution in his voice. "Why do you ask?"

"I wondered if you heard any noises coming from the judge's suite anytime today. Raised voices? Maybe you heard Athena barking?"

"No, I didn't hear anything like that. And I didn't kill the nurse, as I'm going to tell the police during my interview, which I need to get to right now."

Faith winced. She hadn't been at all subtle.

"After that, I'm going to look for Gunther in an effort to keep my job if that's quite all right with you." Cody turned and stormed off down the hallway.

Faith returned to the library. Talking about Cody's criminal past had reminded her of Terrence. Why had he been in court more than once?

The chief had promised to check into Terrence's background, but Faith decided to do a little digging herself. She searched his name and found several articles. The first one covered the lawsuit with Philip.

She found another lawsuit that sounded strikingly familiar. The architect Terrence and his construction company hired to design an office complex claimed that he hadn't been paid for his time and efforts. It seemed as though Terrence might be into some shady business dealings.

Before Faith could read any more articles, her phone rang.

She felt her heart lift when she checked the screen and saw that it was Wolfe.

"I'm sorry I haven't called sooner, but I've been in a meeting," he said. "I just received your texts. Are you all right?"

Faith felt a lump rise in her throat. "It's so good to hear your voice. Finding Diana's body was horrible, but I'm fine."

"What was the cause of death?"

"It looked like she was strangled."

"You don't sound sure," Wolfe said.

Faith drew in a deep breath, then let it out slowly. "I did wonder if the snake had managed to somehow wrap itself around her neck."

"It seems unlikely, but pythons are constrictors. It's possible, I suppose."

"I'm probably letting my imagination run wild. But there was no murder weapon in sight, and as far as I know, they haven't found it yet."

"The investigation has barely started," Wolfe reminded her. "Please promise me you'll be careful until Chief Garris gets to the bottom of this. I want to find you safe and sound when I get back."

Faith promised, and they hung up.

She only hoped being careful would be enough.

The next morning when Faith arrived to open the library, she found a note from Brooke affixed to the door. Her friend wanted to borrow a copy of *The Little House Cookbook* from the library's collection.

Fortunately, that was one of the books from the Laura Ingalls Wilder collection that she had not carried down to the log cabin. She hadn't thought that the memoirists would be interested in cooking anything on the potbellied stove, no matter how enthusiastically they were embracing their experience in the rustic cabin.

Faith retrieved the book and headed off to the kitchen. As she walked along the brightly lit corridor, she flipped through the cookbook's pages with its insightful commentary and charming illustrations of pioneer families and the foods they enjoyed together.

As Faith considered the attention Laura Ingalls Wilder had lavished on descriptions of meals and the ingredients used to make them, she wondered if Brooke wanted to borrow the cookbook because she was planning something special for the writing retreat guests. Knowing Brooke, it was likely she was trying to cheer them up with something extra, as their retreat had been disrupted yesterday by Diana's death and the police investigation, in addition to the missing snake the day before. Of course, it was just as likely Brooke was interested in expanding her repertoire of recipes from an earlier era.

Brooke was a devoted reader of romance novels, many of which were historical fiction. She tended to wax nostalgic to the Candle House Book Club—of which Faith, Eileen, Midge, and Brooke were members—over the techniques and dishes featured in the books. Faith would not have been the least bit surprised if Brooke had been reading a romance set in the pioneering days and wanted to try her hand at a meal that had taken her fancy.

As Faith scanned the cookbook, careful not to trip as she walked, her mind filled with the possibilities. Would Brooke whip up a batch of little cakes made with not much more than cornmeal, salt, and water? What about a special dish made of prairie jackrabbit and white flour dumplings? Not that there was a lot of prairie jackrabbit to be found locally.

Faith supposed Brooke could provide a meal of chicken pie, baked beans, pickled beets, and pumpkin pie, like one of the Sunday dinners mentioned in *Farmer Boy*, the story of Almanzo's childhood on a farm in northern New York.

Just as Faith reached the door that led down to the kitchen, Janine Peters approached her. She wore a blue tracksuit and matching tennis shoes, and her shiny hair was pulled back into a neat, bouncing ponytail. Her expression was one of cheerful determination.

"I'm so glad I ran into you," Janine said. "I wondered if you could answer a question for me."

"Absolutely," Faith said. "What do you need?"

"Do you keep hot-water bottles here?" Janine asked. "I couldn't find one anywhere in our room."

Faith was surprised. Hot-water bottles were not the sort of thing guests generally requested, especially once the weather had turned warm. By May, most people were enjoying the warm spring breezes and had no need for such a thing.

"It's for Philip," Janine explained. "He has terrible allergies, and now he also has an earache. A hot-water bottle usually helps his ears."

"Oh no. I hope Philip wasn't allergic to something in the tunnels."

"I'm afraid he suffers from all sorts of allergies, particularly molds and pollen," Janine said. "It could have come from anywhere. Mr. Jaxon asked him to inspect some of the outbuildings too."

"If I'd known that, I wouldn't have taken him up on his offer to search the tunnels." Faith knew how miserable some people could be when they suffered from spring allergies.

Janine patted her arm. "Don't worry. Philip was looking for an excuse to be allowed to explore down there. If it hadn't been to search for that snake, it would have been something else. He'll always choose the opportunity to explore a fascinating bit of architecture over playing it safe with his allergies."

"I'd be happy to run to the pharmacy in town to pick up some over-the-counter medication," Faith offered. "That way, you won't have to miss more of the scheduled events."

"Thank you, but he has plenty of medicine on hand, especially when he's on a jobsite," Janine replied. "He really only needs the hot-water bottle."

"Check with Ms. Russell or the front desk clerk. They'll make sure you get one. The manor strives to take good care of its guests."

"I'll go to the front desk now. And thanks. Philip will be right as rain in no time."

"He's lucky to have you taking such good care of him," Faith said. Janine smiled.

Once again, Faith was struck by the other woman's appearance of glowing good health. She looked like one of those people who had never been sick a day in her life. Perhaps that was why she was so attentive to her husband's ailments.

"Philip is a wonderful man, and it always pleases me to fuss over him a bit," Janine said. "Besides, he seems to appreciate it. I think it's because he never quite got over the loss of his parents. Now a dose of mothering once in a while makes him feel better."

"That could explain it. Was he very young when he lost them?"

"Philip was in his early teens when both of his parents were killed," Janine answered. "I don't have many of the details because he doesn't like to talk about it."

"Oh, how awful." Faith's heart squeezed.

"Please don't mention it to him. He always says he prefers not to wallow in the past. He doesn't like for people to know because he thinks they'll look at him with pity."

"I certainly won't bring it up to him," Faith said. "Is there anything else I can help you with?"

"You could point me in the direction of the front desk. This place is so big, and I'm all turned around."

Faith laughed. "That's perfectly understandable. I was here for ages before I stopped getting lost." She indicated the direction.

Janine thanked her and trotted away.

As Faith resumed her trek to the kitchen, she wondered about Philip's personal history. What a tragedy that he had lost his parents, especially at such an important stage of his life.

Faith had always been grateful for her own family—even more so when she heard a heartbreaking story like that—and it made her heart hurt to think of anyone growing up without the love and support she had been fortunate enough to experience.

Faith's parents were alive and well, but they lived in Springfield, and she didn't see them as much as she would have liked. After hearing about Philip's situation, however, she was grateful beyond words that she got to see them at all.

Besides, her aunt lived right here in Lighthouse Bay, working as the librarian at the Candle House Library. Even as an adult, Faith found she relied on Eileen in good times as well as bad. She thought about the innumerable ways, both large and small, that her aunt helped her in life, and she resolved to be more mindful in her appreciation of Eileen.

If there was anything she'd learned from Diana's death, it was that tomorrow was never guaranteed.

12

As Faith entered the warm, cheerful kitchen, Brooke gave her the trademark smile that always brightened Faith's day. With her twinkling blue eyes and youthful appearance, Brooke radiated energy and enthusiasm no matter what the circumstances. It was impossible to remain out of sorts around her.

"I see you got my message," Brooke said, pointing to the cookbook tucked under Faith's arm.

"What are you willing to give me in exchange for it?" Faith teased as she walked over to a glass cake stand on the counter. The yellow Bundt cake under the dome was drizzled with pale glaze and looked delicious.

Brooke laughed. "How about a slice of my latest recipe experiment?"

"Sounds like a fair trade," Faith said, handing her friend the cookbook. "How did you know my price?"

"You weren't exactly subtle," Brooke said with a grin. She set the book on the counter, then lifted the dome off the stand.

Faith inhaled deeply. "It smells amazing, but I can't quite put my finger on the fragrance. What's in it?"

Brooke set the book down on the counter. "It's a lemon-lavender cake. I harvested the lavender blossoms myself from the property, then added a lemon glaze. It'll be great with tea."

"Lavender in a cake?" Faith asked. "Isn't lavender for soaps and sachets?"

Brooke cut off a generous slice, placed it on a pretty china plate, and slid it across the counter to Faith with a delicate silver fork. "Yes, but it's also used in baking. It adds a subtle aromatic element that should complement the lemon. The flavor combination makes me think of the English countryside."

"I can't wait to taste it." Faith took her plate to the small table in the corner and sat down. "What made you decide to give it a try?"

"I was inspired when I saw all the lavender in bloom outside."

Faith couldn't help but spare a thought for Gunther as she noticed the lilac-colored flecks and yellow speckles scattered throughout the cake. But when she took a bite, all thoughts of the snake vanished. The brightness of the lemon and the unexpected subtle flavor from the lavender blended together perfectly.

Not for the first time, Faith thought that it was a good thing she took care of the library and Brooke was the one in charge of the food.

"This is absolutely scrumptious," Faith said.

"Oh, I almost forgot the tea." In a flash, Brooke boiled water, then poured it into a beautiful china pot with a special blend of Earl Grey to steep. She placed it on a tray along with a delicate pitcher of milk and a small bowl of sugar cubes. Two teacups, two saucers, and two spoons completed the presentation, which she set on the table with a flourish.

Faith always admired her friend's prowess in the kitchen and the speed with which she whipped up such lovely and thoughtful spreads. The tiny spoons even had the French word for tea, *thé*, etched on the handles in a fancy script.

Brooke grabbed the book from the counter and sat down across from Faith. "I'm so happy that this cookbook was in the library," she said, tapping the cover. "Although I'm not surprised. The library has everything."

"What do you need it for?" Faith asked. "Were you suddenly inspired to whip up a meal featuring salt pork and molasses?"

Brooke laughed. "Close. Pamela asked me if I could plan a dinner around recipes from the Little House on the Prairie series. When I searched online, a review of this cookbook showed up. It's supposed to be historically accurate and also delicious, so I figured any meal from it would be a winner."

"With you in charge of the dinner, I'm sure it'll be fantastic."

Brooke checked the tea to be sure it was sufficiently steeped, then poured two steaming, fragrant cups.

Faith accepted hers and took a sip. The rich taste of Earl Grey accentuated the delicate flavors in the cake. She released a long breath and felt the last knots of stress unravel in her shoulders.

"So, I hear there's been a lot going on upstairs. Have you sent out a distress call to the man in charge?" Brooke winked at her, then sipped her tea.

Faith had grown accustomed to the gentle teasing she received from her friends about her new relationship with Wolfe, but she still felt a rush of warmth to her cheeks. She glanced down at the table and willed the flush to leave her face.

Brooke grinned at her and took a bite of her own cake.

"I think my working relationship with Marlene would suffer if I were to call on Wolfe every time something happened here. It's hard enough to juggle my private and personal lives without complicating things by stepping on Marlene's toes."

"Speak of the devil," Brooke whispered. She raised her eyebrows, her gaze locked on the door behind Faith.

Faith slowly turned to face the door with a sense of dread.

"Taking a break, I see." Marlene crossed the kitchen. The sound of her heels against the floor bounced off the gleaming stainless steel surfaces of the refrigerator and the industrial-size range. She stopped at Faith's side and glared down at the half-eaten piece of cake on the plate in front of her.

"Actually, I asked Faith to bring me a cookbook I'm using to plan the dinner for the writers at the log cabin," Brooke said smoothly. "I didn't have time to run up and get it since I was busy preparing the other meals. I offered her a snack to thank her for dropping it off."

Marlene shifted her gaze to Faith. She narrowed her eyes, and Faith was quite certain the assistant manager was thinking up a new reason to complain.

"Would you like a piece of cake, Marlene?" Brooke offered. "It's a new recipe, and I'd appreciate your opinion."

"Unlike some people, I'm too busy to sit around snacking and chatting all day," Marlene said, then pointed at Faith with a professionally polished nail. "I came in here looking for you, since you weren't at your post."

Faith slid off the stool and pushed away her cup and plate. It had been a lovely break while it had lasted. "What can I do for you?" she said, ensuring her tone remained light and pleasant.

"I've been speaking with Judge Davidson, and the poor man does not feel up to the task of walking his dog regularly," Marlene said. "He believes his heart simply cannot take it, and he doesn't want to risk his health without his personal nurse on hand."

Faith thought the judge had looked well enough when she had seen him arguing with Cody in the hallway. Perhaps physical exertion was more detrimental to his heart condition than emotional upheaval. Or perhaps he didn't get riled up when he distressed other people. She supposed that would be a characteristic that could serve a judge well when it came time to deliver a sentence.

Still, she couldn't help but think that perhaps the judge simply didn't care to walk his dog himself. She stifled a sigh as she realized where Marlene was headed with this conversation.

"Since his nurse is no longer able to walk his dog, he requires someone else to take over the task," Marlene said. "I volunteered you for the job."

"We have plenty of staff in the kennels or the pet spa who could handle it," Faith protested.

"They're all busy watching out for that dreadful snake," Marlene said. "I assured the judge that you would be happy to take over dog-walking duties for the rest of his visit."

Faith felt her spirits begin to flag. She wasn't sure when she would have time to walk Athena in addition to her other responsibilities, and she knew Watson would not be pleased about her spending so much time with another animal who clearly disliked him. But the look on Marlene's face told her that further protesting would do her no good.

"When does he want me to start?" Faith asked, trying to keep the weariness out of her voice.

"You'll have to get in touch with him to work out the details," Marlene said. "I have far too many responsibilities on my plate with Wolfe gone to act as a messenger pigeon for you and a guest."

Faith decided that rather than complaining or taking offense, she would view the responsibility as an opportunity to spend more time outside basking in the beautiful weather. In addition, there was much in bloom in May, and she always enjoyed seeing the gardens.

Faith smiled at Marlene. "I'll speak to the judge and let him know it will be my pleasure to help out."

Marlene's pale-green eyes widened in surprise. She opened her mouth, then snapped it shut again. Without another word, the assistant manager turned on her heel and bolted out the door.

"That really told her," Brooke said. "She was expecting you to put up a fuss, and if I had to guess, I'd say she was looking forward to it."

"Marlene's all right. You know that. It's better to handle her with kindness than to argue."

"Yes, but it's even better to fly under her radar entirely. She seems determined to find fault with you, especially since you and Wolfe started dating."

"Her attitude lately has been putting me in mind of something Pamela said to the memoir writers the other day."

"What was that?" Brooke asked.

"Pamela was telling them that difficult people and challenging circumstances make for the best stories in a memoir," Faith replied. "She encouraged them to think about the people who acted as antagonists in their own life stories."

"Like the villain?"

"The person doesn't have to be exactly villainous. The antagonist simply has a different agenda or goal from the hero of the story. She mentioned Nellie Oleson as an example."

Brooke began to collect the plates and cups. "Wasn't she the girl who spent so much time making Laura's life difficult?"

"That's her," Faith said.

"Then I would say without a doubt that Marlene is your Nellie Oleson," Brooke declared.

"I'm afraid this situation could turn into something much more serious than the tensions between two young girls," Faith said.

"What do you mean?"

Faith frowned. "If Marlene doesn't come to terms with my relationship with Wolfe, I'm not sure the manor will be big enough for the two of us."

Brooke stared at her. "That's a little dark."

"You're right. It was a little more dramatic than I meant to be." Faith frowned. "But I wonder if someone truly felt that way about Diana."

13

Faith left the warmth and friendliness of the kitchen and went in search of the judge. If she had to add walking Athena to her full list of responsibilities, she thought it would be best to find out the details right away so she could prepare.

Before she could track him down, however, a text from the judge appeared on Faith's cell phone screen. *Meet me at the library—where I would have thought the librarian would have been in the first place—ASAP to discuss Athena's schedule.*

Faith attempted to tamp down her annoyance that Marlene had given her private number to a guest and tried to focus on the bright side. At least she didn't have to wander through the manor searching for the man.

Judge Davidson and Athena were waiting for her outside the library door.

"I'm sorry to keep you waiting," Faith said as she unlocked the door and ushered them inside.

He took a seat in front of the fireplace, and the dog jumped into his lap. "Well, I hope you understand what a privilege it is to be entrusted with Athena. I don't allow just anyone to walk her, but Ms. Russell assured me that you would be more than capable of handling this responsibility. So here I am—against my better judgment, I might add."

Keeping a firm hold on her temper, Faith sat down next to him with what she hoped was a reassuring smile. "I'll take care of her as if she were my own."

"You are a cat person, aren't you?" the judge demanded, squinting at her as if anyone who could like cats was highly suspect.

"While my cat, Watson, means the world to me, I love most animals, and I'm sure Athena and I will get along fine."

Athena grunted, which Faith took to mean she was not convinced that Faith was qualified to walk her.

"I suppose you can't be any less suited for it than my nurse was." He rubbed Athena's chin. "The fool woman kept telling me that she was hired to take care of me, not my dog."

"How often does Athena need to be walked?" Faith asked.

"At least five times each day," he answered. "I would do it, but my health prevents me from exerting myself."

"I'm sorry to hear you're so unwell," Faith said.

"I will leave her with you now as I am heading to the cabin to work on my memoir and cannot be disturbed." The judge lifted Athena from his lap and placed her on the floor by his feet. Then he stood.

"I would be happy to take her to the kennels after her walk if you'd like," Faith said, thinking of the work piling up on her desk and in her in-box.

He handed Faith a leash. "I would not like that at all, and neither would Athena. If I thought the kennels were suitable for my dog, I would have arranged for a stay there already."

"I won't be able to return her to you for some time," Faith said. "I have duties to attend to in the library this afternoon." *And my duties have increased.*

"You may keep her with you all afternoon if necessary," the judge said. "But do not drop her off at the kennels like some common mongrel."

"I understand. Is there anything else I should know about her care?" Faith asked.

"I will also expect you to feed and water her, then walk her after dinner and again before bed." He gave the dog a final pat on the head before striding out the door.

Faith could see no reason why the judge couldn't walk Athena to the cabin if he was already going there. She suspected he enjoyed making demands on others and exercising his clout. Faith wondered how Diana had managed to put up with him.

Athena plopped down near the fireplace and stretched out for a nap. Faith couldn't help but laugh. "Make yourself at home."

The cat knew his human had good intentions, but if she honestly thought he was going to stay cooped up in the cottage all day, she didn't know him very well.

He understood that she was worried—he could feel the nerves wound tight inside her. However, as long as he stayed out of her sight, she would be none the wiser, and he could still exercise his natural rights to explore and patrol. He decided to return to the cabin to make a full investigation. From what he'd already seen, it was unlike any other human residence he had encountered.

The cat exited the cottage through one of his many routes—all unknown to his person—and headed toward the scents of freshly cut wood surrounded by grass and trees. The building was new and quite solid, so he had to search for a few minutes before he found a way in.

As he was sniffing along the back wall, a sudden rustling sound outside brought him up short. The cat slipped back out the way he'd come in and crept silently around the cabin until he reached the spot where he'd heard the noise.

A human crouched beside the wall, affixing something to the exterior. After a few moments, the human straightened, nodded in satisfaction, and retreated into the nearby trees.

The grumpy old human who owned the badly behaved dog stumped into view, wheezing, and disappeared inside the cabin.

The cat turned to check on the other human, who was holding something he hadn't noticed before. The human pressed a button on the device, then headed toward the manor.

A sharp smell hit the cat's nostrils. He flattened his ears. It was time to leave.

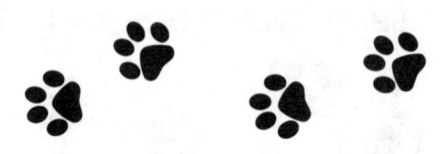

Although Faith had not been eager to keep an eye on the little bulldog, she had to admit that Athena was very well-behaved. The only disturbance she caused was the sound of her asthmatic snoring as she slept before the hearth.

Faith kept her mind on her work as best she could and found the time passed quickly until Athena woke up and walked to the door, where she made whining, snuffling sounds that Faith understood to mean she desired a walk.

Since there were no patrons in the library, Faith snapped Athena's leash onto her collar, locked the door, and headed out into the garden.

As Faith strolled along with the dog, she felt glad to be outside enjoying the gorgeous gardens that were expertly tended by the manor's gardeners. Crab apple and pear trees bloomed profusely. Every now and again, a delicate pink petal fluttered on the breeze in front of them. Faith inhaled the twin scents of peonies and salty ocean air.

Athena seemed to be enjoying herself too. The dog stopped frequently to sniff the ornate brickwork paths and the bark mulch tidily blanketing the neat garden beds. But then she started to dig.

"Athena, no!" Faith tugged her away from the flower bed and looked her over in dismay. The dog's front paws were muddy, and there were bits of dirt and mulch clinging to her muzzle. She didn't want Athena to get any dirtier or damage the flowers, so she urged her along toward the open spaces of the grounds. As much as Faith enjoyed the gardens, they were clearly no place for a dog who seemed to have an affinity for the art of excavation.

Up ahead, Faith spotted Philip, Janine, and Pamela heading toward the log cabin. She was trying to decide whether to call out to them when a gray squirrel appeared in the space between the visitors and Faith and Athena.

The little dog stopped inspecting a stand of white birches and lunged for the squirrel.

Faith was not prepared for the sudden movement, and the leash slipped from her hands as Athena bolted. Faith gave a shout.

The group ahead of them spun around, then took off after the short-legged dog.

Faith had felt sorry for Athena because of her breathing difficulties, but now she was grateful that the dog was not athletic.

Athena had not gone very far when Philip flung himself on the leash trailing behind her, bringing her to a sudden halt.

Faith smiled at him as she approached. "Thank you so much. I don't know what I would have done if I had lost her."

"I can't see the judge being merciful to someone who let Athena escape." Philip chuckled as he handed Faith the leash.

She wrapped it around her wrist several times before she felt confident that the dog would not get away from her again.

"I think it would be best if none of us let him know what happened," Janine said.

Pamela nodded. "From what I've seen of the stories the judge plans to include in his memoir, he hasn't exactly been known for his mercy, and he seems to pride himself on that."

Just then, Terrence appeared in a gap between two spruce trees. He strode over to join them.

"Are you ready for the next writing session?" Pamela asked him.

"Raring to go," Terrence said. If he had any simmering animosity toward the judge or anyone else, it didn't show. He seemed content and relaxed. Faith was glad that someone felt that way.

"Wonderful." Pamela beamed. "Let's get started. Faith, why don't you come with us? I'm guessing Athena won't mind a longer walk."

Though she wasn't sure how the judge would feel about her arrival, Faith agreed, and the entire group continued across the field.

The steady breeze brought a mixture of smells toward Faith. No longer was the scent of garden flowers in the air but rather that of damp earth, freshly mown grass, and something more elusive.

As they drew closer to the log cabin, Faith realized what the unidentified smell was.

Smoke.

14

Faith glanced at Pamela, who seemed to have recognized the smell of smoke too.

Without a word, they both broke into a run and made a beeline for the log cabin. Athena somehow managed to keep up.

As they came closer to the rustic structure, Faith noticed the smell of smoke had intensified. Hungry orange flames licked the base of the cabin all around the perimeter. Faith quickly tied Athena's leash to a rail on the covered wagon before turning back to the fire.

Janine and Philip reached the cabin as Faith and Pamela raced up the porch steps.

Faith gingerly placed her hand on the metal door latch. It felt slightly warm to the touch, but the rest of the door did not seem hot. She lifted the collar of her shirt over her nose and mouth and took a deep breath as she pressed down on the latch and slowly opened the door.

The judge stood in the center of the smoke-filled room, clutching his chest. The same look was on his face that Faith had seen the day before during his angina attack.

Faith held her breath as she entered the cabin. The smell of smoke was overwhelming, and the temperature made sweat break out on her forehead almost immediately.

She hurried toward the judge, grasping him firmly by the arm. Philip rushed to his other side, and the two of them helped the judge safely out of the building. They eased him down onto a grassy spot well away from the cabin and the fire.

Janine and Terrence worked together to dip buckets of water from a seasonal stream that ran through the field near the cabin.

The judge was having trouble catching his breath as he fumbled with the pocket of his sooty linen jacket.

Faith realized he was searching for his angina pills. "Do you need me to get your pill bottle for you?"

The judge nodded.

Faith reached into his jacket pocket and found the plastic container. She lifted it out, popped off the top, and shook a pill into his open palm. Then Faith untied Athena from the covered wagon and led the dog over to the judge so the animal could comfort him.

After asking Pamela to keep an eye on the judge and Athena, Faith rushed to help douse the remaining flames. Then she phoned Marlene to report the incident.

"I'll call the fire department and ask them to come by anyway," Marlene said. "Even if the danger has passed, we need them to investigate the cause of the blaze. I'm counting on you to handle things until they arrive." She hung up abruptly.

Faith slid her phone into her pocket, then examined the log cabin. She was relieved to see that there appeared to be no real damage. Perhaps the logs were still too green to catch fire easily.

"You're lucky we all got here when we did," Terrence told the judge, "and that Pamela had buckets in that covered wagon of hers."

Faith glanced at the judge, who seemed to have recovered from his attack, and shuddered to think what might have happened to him.

"I'm so relieved everyone's okay," Janine said.

Philip nodded. "What I want to know is how the fire started in the first place."

"There's no electricity in the cabin," Pamela reminded them. "And I went in and checked the stove. It's cold, so no one started a fire in it."

"It's not as though the cabin was struck by lightning on a sunny day," Terrence said.

"I suppose it could have been someone who smokes." Philip frowned. "Maybe someone was wandering around the grounds and tossed a smoldering cigarette butt toward the cabin without thinking."

Faith didn't hear much conviction in his voice. Her heart went out to Philip. He'd designed and supervised the building of this log cabin, and now they had to consider the possibility that someone had tried to burn it down.

"I don't remember seeing anyone smoking this week, do you?" Pamela asked the group.

"Fiona read from her memoir the last time we met, and she described in detail a fire-swallowing trick that was part of her repertoire," Terrence answered. "Maybe she and that assistant of hers were practicing the trick down here."

Everyone glanced around as though searching for clues, but no one found anything—no cigarette butts or magician's paraphernalia.

And where were Fiona and Cody anyway? If the group was meeting at the log cabin, why weren't they here? Maybe Cody wouldn't be in attendance, but Faith found it strange that Fiona was missing.

Faith walked around the back of the building. A small charred spot that appeared darker than the rest of the logs caught her attention. She crept closer to the building and bent over an area located about a foot up on the side of the structure. The grass beneath the darkened spot seemed to be even more charred than the surrounding vegetation.

She was not an expert on fire by any measure, but she found it curious that one area seemed more affected than the rest of the building. Was this the origin of the blaze? Had it been arson? Faith shook her head. She would have to leave that determination to the professionals. It was no good borrowing trouble, especially when there had been more than enough trouble lately.

She noticed that there were no tools or building materials left over from the construction of the cabin. The builders had done a great job of creating the illusion that the cabin had simply sprung up out of nowhere. The only signs that someone had recently been here were the patches of trampled grass, where the impromptu bucket brigade had walked around the cabin to put out the fire.

A cold feeling settled in the pit of her stomach. Faith crossed her arms over her chest as a cloud passed over the sun and temporarily bathed the field in shadow.

She couldn't help but think there was something ominous at work at the manor. There had been so many incidents in such a short time—Gunther going missing, Diana's death, and now this fire. Were they all accidents, or was something sinister going on? Faith was definitely leaning toward the latter, but if there was some connection, she couldn't see it.

Faith returned to the front of the cabin and waited with the others. The mood was somber, and everyone was quiet.

Soon the fire department arrived. The officials determined that the structure was safe, but they couldn't verify the cause of the fire until they had performed a more in-depth investigation.

Faith called Marlene to give her the news. As soon as she disconnected, she saw Pamela addressing the group.

"If you're all still up for it, we'll have to move today's writing session to the manor," Pamela said.

The others agreed, and they took off in that direction.

Faith approached the judge. "Would you like me to get you a ride to the manor? I can ask one of the groundskeepers to bring a golf cart."

He waved his hand dismissively. "No, I'll walk. And I'll keep Athena with me."

Faith walked several paces behind them to make sure they arrived safely at the manor, then returned to the library.

She sat down at her desk and texted Wolfe with the news. She assumed he was in a meeting and wouldn't be able to respond right away, but she wanted to let him know.

Marlene stopped by a little later. "Tonight's dinner will proceed as planned."

"Really?" Faith couldn't hide her surprise. The dinner was scheduled to take place at the cabin, and she'd assumed it would be canceled or the venue would at least be changed because of the fire.

Marlene nodded. "Since the fire department has deemed the cabin safe and it's relatively undamaged, Ms. Browning insists on going ahead with the dinner there. However, because of the ongoing investigation, the meal will be held outside, and no one is to go too near the cabin. Fortunately, it's supposed to be a mild night."

Faith was surprised at Pamela's insistence, especially because the group leader had moved the location of the earlier workshop from the cabin to the manor.

Without waiting for a response, Marlene left.

Almost as soon as Faith returned to work, she received a text from the judge, asking her to walk Athena. Faith would have thought the dog had had plenty of exercise recently, but apparently she was wrong.

She went upstairs to the Charles Dickens Suite and knocked.

The judge opened the door with the bulldog at his side. "I'm glad you're here. Athena's ready to go," he said, holding out the dog's leash. "Bring her back when you're done."

The judge seemed to be in surprisingly good spirits after the loss of his nurse, two angina attacks, and a dramatic rescue from a fire.

Faith took the leash. "You seem to be doing well. Are you planning to hire another nurse?"

"No, I don't need anyone else. I'm capable of taking care of myself."

Faith wasn't sure she agreed with his decision, but it wasn't her place to say so. "I hope you at least plan to take it easy before the dinner at the log cabin this evening. After all, you did have another angina attack earlier."

"I don't need to rest. I intend to work on my memoir." He waved her off and shut the door.

Faith and Athena rambled across the grounds for a little while. When Faith returned Athena to the judge, he took the dog and closed the door.

The library was fairly quiet, and the rest of the afternoon passed without further incident, thank goodness. She even managed to cross a few items off her to-do list. Finally, it was time to lock up and return to her cottage to change for the evening.

Watson greeted her when she opened the front door. He brushed against her legs and purred loudly.

"I'm glad to see you too," she said. "I've missed you. Thank you for staying here today."

Before getting ready for dinner, she took a few minutes to sit on the couch with Watson perched on her lap, giving her purr therapy while she gave him a thorough scratching.

Her phone buzzed, and she smiled when she glanced at the screen. It was Wolfe.

"I'm sorry that I couldn't get back to you sooner," he said. "I saw your text about the fire at the log cabin. Are you all right?"

"I'm fine. Fortunately, there wasn't much damage."

"So the fire department couldn't determine the cause of the fire?" Wolfe asked.

"No, they need to do a more thorough investigation." Faith paused before adding, "I'm concerned that it might be arson."

"Let's hope not," he replied. "I don't understand why anyone would want to burn down the cabin."

They talked a few more minutes about all that had happened since the retreat started. Too soon it was time for Faith to get ready, and they said their goodbyes.

Faith gently moved Watson from her lap and went to her bedroom.

When she had been asked to participate in what had promised to be an entertaining and unusual event, she'd been excited. But now, she dressed for the occasion with no small amount of reluctance. As she pulled a borrowed sprig-printed prairie skirt from her closet, she considered everything she knew.

Diana had clearly been strangled, but they didn't yet know how or by whom—or what. Had the nurse been the victim of a snake attack or something far more sinister?

And what about Gunther's disappearance? It was impossible for the snake to have slithered out of his terrarium without moving the latch or disturbing the weighted lid, so it was clear he'd been deliberately set loose.

Faith was certain the judge's heart condition was not the fault of another. But she was not so sure about the fire at the log cabin. If it had been set intentionally, she wondered if the arsonist realized there'd been someone inside. Had the arsonist known the judge was inside? Had he been a target? The man undoubtedly had enough enemies.

She considered the possible suspects. Janine, Philip, and Pamela had all been in plain view when Faith first smelled the smoke emanating from the log cabin. Terrence had joined them almost immediately, but Faith could not say for sure if he'd had enough time to set the fire before meeting them at the edge of the field.

Where had the others been? Cody, Fiona, and Christina had not been accounted for just before the blaze was noticed. Any of them could have had good reason to want to see harm come to Judge Davidson. As much as Faith hated to think any of them capable of doing such a terrible thing, she had to include them on her mental list of possible arson suspects.

Watson meowed, interrupting her thoughts.

Faith quickly finished getting ready, then filled Watson's bowl with his favorite food and stayed with him while he ate it. She hated to leave him at home again, but the kitchen clock said it was time to go.

With a heavy heart, she left the cottage and made her way to the log cabin.

As she trudged along the path, she wondered if she was about to dine with a snake thief, an arsonist, or a killer.

Or all three.

15

Despite her misgivings about the log cabin as a location for the dinner after the earlier incident, Faith had to admit the scene was charming.

Kerosene lanterns hung from shepherd's hooks strategically placed around the field and in front of the log cabin. Vases of wildflowers graced the steps of the porch and a long, wooden table, where the guests were enjoying their dinner under the stars. The covered wagon was parked nearby, but Faith didn't see Stormy. She assumed the horse was at the stables.

The air was filled with the delicious scents of the food Brooke had prepared, and Faith felt her spirits lift. She hurried to join the group.

Brooke stood behind a smaller table that was covered with platters of food.

Faith went over to her friend and greeted her.

"I heard about the fire," Brooke whispered. "What happened?"

"They're not sure yet," Faith answered quietly. "It might have been arson."

Brooke raised her eyebrows. "Who would do such a thing?"

"I don't know." Faith glanced at the guests, not wanting anyone to overhear their conversation. "Let's discuss it later."

Brooke nodded, then gestured to the platters of ham, corn bread, pickles, salt pork, and sautéed greens. "Help yourself."

"Everything looks wonderful," Faith said as she filled a blue enamel plate. She thanked Brooke and joined the guests at the other table.

Janine, Philip, and Pamela sat on one side of the table. Terrence, Christina, Cody, and Fiona were seated on the other side.

Faith slipped into one of the two open seats between Pamela and Janine. As she listened to the chatter of the other guests, she realized someone was missing. "Where's the judge?" she asked. "Did he not feel well enough to join us this evening?"

"He didn't send any word one way or the other," Pamela answered. "At least not to me."

Faith glanced at the other diners.

They all shook their heads.

"After the incident earlier, I wouldn't be surprised if he decided he'd had enough excitement for one day," Janine said. "He's not a young man, and his health is anything but good."

"It would take more than a little scare to do away with him," Terrence said, then turned to Philip and grinned. "Am I right?"

Philip grimaced as he set his fork down on the table. "I can't say I've given the judge all that much thought, and I don't intend to do so now." He picked up his fork and tucked back into Brooke's delicious cooking with gusto.

Janine patted her husband's hand and gave him a supportive smile.

"I'm glad the judge isn't here," Christina admitted. "Earlier when he saw me with Prunella, he said he couldn't understand why I'd be so devoted to a little rat like her. It hurt her feelings. I had to take her to the spa and get her claws painted before she perked up again. He's not a pleasant man."

"I don't think any of us are overly concerned about the party suffering from his absence." Fiona lifted the edge of her veil and maneuvered a forkful of sautéed greens underneath it.

Faith was impressed by how gracefully the magician consumed her food without allowing the slightest glimpse of her face behind the veil's billowing folds.

"In fact, I think we'd all be happier if the judge took to his bed for the rest of the retreat," Fiona added.

The words were harsh, but Faith noticed that everyone except Pamela nodded in agreement.

"Please remember that we all have a story to tell and a different perspective on life," Pamela piped up. "I know that many of you have a reason to resent Judge Davidson, but I hope that it will not spoil anyone's enjoyment of our time together."

"I'm afraid you're asking a great deal," Fiona said, pinching off a bite of corn bread. "Did you know that he presided over the case involving my accident?"

"No, I was not aware of that," Pamela said. "Under the circumstances, I'm sure it must be very difficult for you to interact with him at this retreat."

"Everything is difficult for me under the circumstances," Fiona said, holding up a gloved hand and waving it at the assembled group. "As far as anyone knew, I had an open-and-shut case. And yet the judge ruled in the defendant's favor."

"I remember that everyone was stunned by the outcome of your lawsuit," Janine said.

"That's what my lawyer said," Fiona responded.

"What do you think happened?" Christina asked.

"I believe the judge was paid off," Fiona said, her voice trembling with rage.

Faith barely stifled a gasp of surprise.

"I said so at the time, and I still say so today," Fiona went on. "Not only that, but I think he took my snake. I don't know where he's got Gunther, or who he paid to take him, but I wouldn't put anything past that horrible man."

Faith studied the expressions of the other guests. While she had expected to see surprise, instead she saw several members of the group nodding.

"There are a lot of rumors about the judge's conduct and possible abuses of power over the years," Terrence said. "But I've never been able to prove anything."

"No one's ever been able to prove anything," Fiona said. Her tone grew cold. "It's a shame that neither his heart condition nor the fire this afternoon did away with him."

Even though Fiona's expression was still shrouded by the heavy veil, Faith got the impression that the magician meant every word she said.

"It sounds as if some of you have a good antagonist for your memoirs," Pamela suggested. "Be sure to record how you felt when you dealt with the judge, as well as how you're feeling now. You can also study him this week to make sure you portray him accurately in your books."

The facilitator expertly guided the conversation to the finer points of memoir writing, which naturally came back to Laura Ingalls Wilder and how she had successfully portrayed more than her own youth. "Laura seemed to have a fascination with her husband's boyhood on a prosperous farm."

Pamela pointed out that the book *Farmer Boy* devoted a great deal of space to lovingly cataloging meals consumed by the Wilder family. It seemed as though his experience had been far pleasanter than Laura's own, and she had enjoyed chronicling it for future generations.

"Many of the savory dishes that we've enjoyed this evening were inspired by meals mentioned in the book," Pamela said. "Perhaps Miss Milner could tell us a little about the recipes she used."

"I'd be happy to," Brooke said, stepping forward. "I chose recipes that I thought would both appeal to contemporary diners and also represent foods that the Wilder family would have eaten regularly."

"I had no idea greens could be so delicious," Janine said. "They have this wonderful smoky flavor."

"That's the salt pork, which is similar to bacon. After we fried the pork, we used the same pan to sauté the greens," Brooke said. "Earlier generations were not worried about cholesterol levels in their food. Instead, they were more concerned about getting enough to eat."

"Working on a farm probably meant they weren't worried about consuming too many calories," Terrance said as he patted his stomach.

"I'm sure you're right," Pamela said. "Shall we give Miss Milner a round of applause to show our appreciation for the wonderful meal?"

Faith was delighted to see her friend receive some well-deserved accolades for her culinary skills.

Brooke nodded her thanks, then set about plating the dessert course. Soon she passed around generous slices of apple pie with homemade ice cream.

The conversation was pleasant as they enjoyed the treat. No one mentioned the judge again.

After the group had finished eating dessert and Brooke had packed away the leftover food, everyone drifted toward the manor.

"You can head back," Pamela told Faith. "The fire marshal gave me permission to go into the cabin and collect some materials I need for my workshops tomorrow."

"Do you need any help?" Faith asked her.

Pamela smiled. "Yes, thank you."

Was it Faith's imagination, or did Pamela seem relieved to have the company? Faith didn't blame her. She wouldn't have been eager to remain on her own out here after the log cabin fire.

Even the covered wagon that had seemed so charming when Pamela had first arrived took on an eerie quality. The wind rippled through the canvas covering and the wooden sides, and the wheels creaked. The temperature started dipping as they slipped into the dark cabin.

To shake off her feeling of unease, Faith turned the conversation toward the facilitator's professional interest. "How did you happen to have the idea to hold a retreat for memoir writers at the manor? It seems like such an inspired idea."

Pamela paused and looked at Faith. "I'd like to take credit for the idea, but it really wasn't mine."

"Whose idea was it?" Faith asked in surprise.

"I don't actually know. I gave a workshop some time ago in the greater Boston area, and it came up there."

"You can't remember who mentioned it to you?"

"I never knew whose idea it was," Pamela said. "At the end of the workshop, I passed out course evaluations for the attendees to fill out and mail back to me later. The last question asked for recommendations for additional workshops, and someone suggested a retreat about writing memoirs. I thought it was a wonderful idea."

"But you never knew who wrote that on their questionnaire?" Faith said. Was it merely coincidence that these people with their intertwined histories had ended up in the same writing group? Or had someone planned it that way? The idea sent a chill down her spine.

"I always ask that the questionnaires be completed anonymously so that people are more comfortable giving their honest evaluation," Pamela said. "I never want anyone to feel constrained about their feedback."

"Did they suggest holding it here at the manor specifically, or was it a general suggestion to hold a retreat about writing memoirs?"

"The person suggested Castleton Manor and mentioned the log cabin project that Mr. Jaxon had commissioned," Pamela said. "I agreed that it seemed like a perfect match, so I suggested it to the other facilitators when we were planning the event." She shrugged. "The rest is history."

"Is this the first time you've met these writers?" Faith asked.

"Oh no," Pamela said. "As a matter of fact, I met Janine, Terrence, the judge, and Fiona at that Boston workshop."

"Were you aware of any hostilities between them back then?" Faith asked.

"I can't say that I was," Pamela said. "But the group was much larger and the workshop lasted for only one day."

"So it would have been easy for them not to interact with each other?" Faith asked.

Pamela nodded.

"How did your small group find out about this particular retreat?" Faith asked.

"I have everyone's contact information from the classes I've offered in the past, and I sent out an e-mail about this opportunity once the plans were finalized," Pamela said. "I expect that's how they heard about it."

As they stepped outside, Faith wondered how each of the attendees would rate this retreat, given everything that had gone on and the decidedly hostile atmosphere. Her thoughts turned once more to the judge and his capacity for riling up the others by his mere presence, not to mention his words.

Pamela scanned the area and shivered. "I think everything's ready for tomorrow, but I want to grab a shawl before we walk back to the manor. It's gotten a little chilly this evening."

Faith agreed and was glad she'd brought her own shawl to wear over her cotton blouse. Spring evenings on the New England coast tended to cool off quite a bit. She pulled her shawl out of her tote bag and wrapped it around her shoulders.

It was more than the anticipated cool evening air that had prompted Faith to bring the delicate wool shawl she wore with her ensemble. It had been knit for her by Eileen, and she often wore it more for emotional comfort than for the need for warmth. She wrapped it a bit tighter and enjoyed the sensation as she waited.

Pamela scrambled up the steps at the back of the wagon and slipped between the flaps in the canvas covering.

And let out a bloodcurdling scream.

16

Faith sprinted to the covered wagon. She raced up the wooden steps, jerked open the flaps of canvas covering the wagon, and clambered inside.

Pamela leaned over a figure slumped against the side of the wagon. It was the judge.

Pamela turned toward her, eyes wide with shock.

Faith approached them. "Judge Davidson, can you hear me?"

The judge remained motionless.

With a sick, sinking feeling, Faith pressed two fingers against his neck and checked for a pulse. Even before she focused on trying to feel for the gentle throbbing that would signal his heartbeat, she knew that her actions were futile. The judge's skin was far too cool for a living man.

"He's gone," Faith said quietly. "There's nothing we can do for him." She grabbed a quilt lying on a bench and covered his body with it. "Let's step outside."

Pamela seemed only too eager to comply and quickly led the way out of the wagon and into the cool evening air.

Faith joined her on the grass near the wagon. She removed her phone from her pocket and dialed 911, then called Marlene.

"Is he really dead?" Pamela asked.

"I believe so."

Pamela took a step backward and almost lost her balance in her haste to move away from the wagon. Her face turned white. "Do we need to stay here with the judge's body until help arrives?"

"I think that would be best," Faith said gently. "I wouldn't feel right about leaving him here alone." She glanced around. Based on the temperature of the judge's skin, she thought he'd been dead for hours, which meant that the killer would be long gone. She figured they'd be safer here than walking back to the manor, although she couldn't be certain.

Pamela's expression said she wanted to put as much distance between herself and the judge's body as possible. In fact, the poor woman looked as though she might faint.

She'll have much to include in her own memoir after this week. Faith pushed the errant thought away and focused on the situation. She started walking toward the wagon.

"What are you doing?" Pamela asked. She stared at the covered wagon as if she expected something to come out of it.

"I'm going to have a quick look around," Faith said, climbing the steps. "I'll be right back."

As Faith entered the wagon, she pulled her shawl more tightly around her shoulders and felt grateful once more for the comfort it provided. The light was rapidly fading, and she scanned the space for some source of light.

An old kerosene lantern hung from a hook screwed into one of the support braces over which the canvas was stretched. She was about to reach up and pluck it from its place when she thought better of it. It would be best not to touch anything before the police arrived, and she didn't have a match anyway. All the lanterns outside had already been extinguished, so those would be no help. And she didn't want to use up her cell phone battery using it as a flashlight.

While the light remained strong enough to see, Faith knelt over the judge's body once more, taking care not to touch him. Even in the gathering gloom inside the covered wagon, Faith could clearly make out a wide discoloration encircling the judge's throat. It matched the mark she had seen on Diana's neck.

Faith's heart hammered in her chest, and blood roared in her ears so loudly it blotted out the sounds of the birds calling to each other from the trees outside. She no longer heard the sound of the breeze rustling through the leaves or the ever-present murmur of the sea.

She was torn between two conflicting and equally terrifying thoughts. Had Gunther managed to escape from the manor and make his way down to the log cabin site? Or had the mark on the judge's neck been made by a two-legged predator? Neither scenario brought Faith any comfort as she considered the possibilities.

Another disturbing thought struck her: If Gunther was responsible for strangling the judge, was he still hidden somewhere inside the wagon?

Faith assessed the situation, starting by examining the covered wagon. She had not been inside the wagon since Pamela's arrival. She had only enjoyed a ride on the driver's seat with Pamela the day she had pulled up to the log cabin.

As she studied the interior, Faith thought she would have found the wagon delightful under any other circumstances. Pamela had outfitted it with many of the comforts of home.

At the far end, she had positioned a double mattress on top of the platform. A homey patchwork quilt was spread over it and tucked in neatly to hold it in place. Several plump pillows graced one end of the mattress, and a cozy buffalo-check throw was draped across the other.

Stationed in front of the bed on either side were built-in benches with cushions on top of them. The judge sat semi-upright on one of them. His body was slumped over to lean against the foot of the bed. In between the benches, beneath the bed platform, Faith noticed a door that she guessed led to storage.

A bank of wooden cubbies containing several wicker baskets stood along one wall. Faith noticed papers in one. Another held a few skeins of green yarn, a pair of long metal knitting needles, and a partially finished project.

On the left, a sheaf of papers and a pen rested on top of a deep shelf built into the wall. A wooden stool sat tucked beneath the shelf. Faith assumed it was Pamela's makeshift desk.

Finally, Faith concluded it was unlikely that Gunther was still in the wagon. He was simply too large to be hiding in this compact space, and she doubted very much that he could have entered the storage area under the bed and pulled the door shut behind him.

Then Faith realized that the snake could be lurking underneath the wagon. She let out a small sigh of relief as she immediately rejected the idea. In light of what the animal control officer had told her, she really didn't think the reptile would endure the cool, damp evening outdoors on the coast of Massachusetts. As a cold-blooded creature, Gunther was far more likely to be holed up somewhere warmer for the night.

She set aside her thoughts of Gunther for the moment and considered the possibility of a human perpetrator. Faith had not seen the judge since earlier that day when she'd taken Athena for another walk. She had suggested that the judge rest before dinner, but he'd refused and said he intended to work on his memoir instead.

What had brought the judge to the covered wagon, and when had he entered it? When was the last time that Pamela had been inside the wagon?

She heard the sound of sirens approaching in the distance.

Suddenly an even more distressing thought occurred to her. Had Pamela really been as surprised as she'd seemed when she discovered the judge's body?

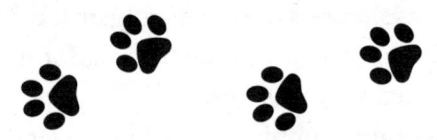

As soon as his human came home, the cat realized she was unhappy. He didn't know exactly what had happened to cause her to worry, but he intended to comfort her. He rubbed his head against her legs, but he couldn't help but notice it did little to change her mood. It would take more than his attention to help her, which meant the situation was truly dire.

All night long he watched her toss and turn as she slept. Something was very wrong.

The cat was determined to make her feel better. Now he just had to figure out how to do it.

When the light rose in the sky, his person got up and prepared to go to the manor. She fed him and herself, but the cat had the distinct impression that she was doing it all in a kind of haze.

As his person opened the door, the cat slipped past her and outside before she could attempt to trap him in the cottage. He would not let her go to the manor alone again. The dewy grass drenched his paws as he raced ahead of her across the garden, and his human called out to him several times, but he ignored both.

Whatever was wrong, it was something beyond her capabilities to handle. It was high time he got involved, and the first step was to investigate whatever was going on at the manor.

As soon as they entered the building, the cat darted away. His human was immediately beset by other humans asking her questions of some kind, and she was unable to follow him. He was grateful for their distraction.

If he was going to help his person, he would need to be clever about it. This was no normal situation that only required him to curl up in her lap and purr. It would take far more than that to fix what was bothering her.

But first he had to find out what that was.

17

Watson slipped out of the cottage before Faith could stop him. He ran ahead of her to the manor, then disappeared inside when she opened the door.

With Gunther still on the loose, she was terrified for her cat. But before she could track him down, a couple of the guests stopped her to ask questions about the judge.

After she'd answered their questions the best she could, she set out in search of Watson. When she couldn't find him, she checked her watch. It was getting late, and she needed to open the library.

As she strode through the lobby, Christina rushed over and grabbed her arm. "Have you seen Prunella?"

"I'm afraid not," Faith said, feeling a sinking sensation.

"I can't find her," Christina said in a quavering voice.

Faith couldn't believe there was another lost pet. At least a guinea pig was far less disturbing than a ten-foot snake.

Christina wiped her eyes. "I'm worried sick."

Faith guided Christina over to a chair, then dug around in her pocket and pulled out a packet of tissues and offered one to the distressed woman.

Christina accepted it and delicately dabbed at her eyes.

"Where did you last see Prunella?" Faith asked, sitting down next to her.

"I had her with me in the conservatory," Christina said. "It was so warm and pleasant in there, and the plants made it seem like the great outdoors."

"Did she manage to slip out of your arms?" Faith asked, remembering how Christina frequently carried the small creature.

"No. She has a clear plastic ball that I put her in so she can safely explore her environment," Christina said. "I placed her in it and set her down in one of the garden beds. I thought she'd like to roll around between the plants."

"What happened?"

Her face was a picture of guilt. "I went to grab a cup of coffee. I thought she'd be fine by herself for a moment."

"And she wasn't there when you got back?" Faith prompted.

"I couldn't find her anywhere," Christina said, her voice breaking.

"When was this?"

"I'm not sure since I was so upset." Tears began to cascade down Christina's cheeks. "But it wasn't that long ago."

Faith's heart ached at the sight of Christina's tear-streaked face. If Watson had been the missing pet, Faith knew she would have been equally upset. "Have you informed the assistant manager, Ms. Russell? She'll be able to help you."

Christina shook her head.

"Have you asked anyone else if they've seen Prunella recently?" Faith questioned.

"No, I thought I'd speak to you first," Christina said.

"Why me?"

"Because your cat is probably responsible for her disappearance." Now Christina's tone was mildly accusing.

"Watson has been coming to work with me ever since I started my job here," Faith said evenly, though she felt offended on her cat's behalf. "I can assure you that he has never harmed any of our animal guests."

"There's a first time for everything," Christina argued. "I don't care how well-behaved he is. You can't go against an animal's nature. Your cat probably entered the conservatory and made off with Prunella, exercise ball and all. Who else besides a cat would be interested in a guinea pig?"

"I highly doubt he could be responsible. For one thing, we only arrived a few minutes ago," Faith said. "Watson might have batted the plastic ball around, but he couldn't carry it away and hide it somewhere for later."

"Well, she didn't just vanish. If your cat isn't responsible, then where is she?"

"Are you sure she's not hidden under some of the plants?" Faith said. "Or maybe she rolled out the door and into another room."

"I would have seen or heard her if she had rolled into the hallway," Christina said. "How could I have not noticed her while I was getting my coffee at the beverage station?"

Faith wasn't so sure. She knew exactly which beverage station Christina had used. It was tucked into an alcove, and Faith could well imagine how a guinea pig could have rolled down the hall without attracting Christina's notice if she'd been busy pouring and stirring her coffee.

"Did you see any other pets in the conservatory before you left to get your coffee?" Faith asked.

"Of course I didn't," Christina snapped. "If I had seen any other animals in there, I never would have left my Prunella alone to be toyed with. Or worse."

As Faith considered Christina's words, an even more upsetting thought occurred to her. Although she was certain Watson had nothing to do with the guinea pig's disappearance, it was possible that another animal visitor had taken an interest in Prunella.

Could the python have been lurking nearby and snatched up the unprotected little animal, plastic ball and all? The animal control officer had said that the snake would like sunny places, and the conservatory was the sunniest room in the manor.

As Faith imagined the layout and the features of the conservatory, she realized how easy it would be for a small creature like Prunella to become hidden among the lush plants. The sound of the waterfall could have easily masked any noise her exercise ball made as it rolled along the garden beds or even along the paths.

She decided to ask a few more questions before mentioning the possibility that Gunther had somehow been involved in Prunella's disappearance. Christina was upset enough without a horrible theory like that being presented. "Did you see anyone else in the room?"

"No one. That was one of the reasons I decided to stop in the conservatory. I wanted to have a few minutes alone with Prunella."

Faith wondered if Christina's husband had contributed to her desire for some quiet time with her pet. If so, Faith couldn't blame her. Based on Faith's limited interactions with Terrence, he seemed like a difficult man.

"Is it hard to open the plastic ball?" Faith asked.

"You have to put your fingers in the indents of the lid and twist it," Christina answered. "It's secure enough for her to roll around without it opening by accident."

So it was unlikely any animal had removed the lid. Faith wondered if a python would be able to wrap itself around the ball and break it. What about its jaws? Pythons probably had the same ability to swallow large objects that so many snakes shared. Would it ingest a plastic ball if it held a small creature that was similar to those in its usual diet? Faith felt her palms begin to sweat even thinking of the possibility that the poor little guinea pig might be trapped inside Gunther.

"Would the ball open under pressure?" Faith asked. "Or by being jarred in some way?"

Christina raised her eyebrows. "What do you mean by pressure?"

"Like from a sudden drop or if it was squeezed."

"I doubt it. Besides, the garden bed where I put her was at the same level as the surrounding floor. And I left the door open when I went to fetch the coffee, so I'm sure her exercise ball wasn't trapped between the door and the jamb."

Faith couldn't be more specific without terrifying Christina, so she had to keep brainstorming. Had Prunella simply rolled off somewhere and gotten stuck? Or had something far more distressing happened to her? If so, had she been harmed by a hungry python or an unattended four-legged guest, or had one of the human guests caused her disappearance?

This speculation wouldn't help, and she was definitely late opening the library now. "I'm so sorry, but I'm needed at the library. I hope you locate Prunella soon. In the meantime, I strongly recommend that you mention your concerns to the assistant manager right away."

Christina shot to her feet. "Since you obviously don't have the time to help me, I suppose I'll have to do that. And I'll be sure to mention to your boss that your cat is the main suspect in Prunella's disappearance."

As soon as Faith opened the library, she texted Wolfe to tell him about the judge's death.

This was the first time she'd had a chance to contact him. It had been a late night with the EMTs and another police investigation. She'd also deposited Athena at the kennels, despite the late judge's wishes. The dog was perfectly safe and comfortable there, and it wasn't as if Faith could take her to the cottage. Given Athena's dislike of Watson, Faith wouldn't have gotten any sleep.

Not that she'd gotten much anyway.

She glanced up from her phone when someone entered the library.

"Good morning," Janine said flatly. The woman's generally upbeat demeanor was gone. In fact, she looked downright dejected. Her shoulders slumped, and her ponytail even seemed to have lost some of its energetic bounce.

"You don't seem quite like yourself this morning," Faith remarked. "Is something wrong?"

Janine sighed. "I had such high hopes for this getaway, but I think they were misplaced."

Faith could understand if Janine considered the trip a disaster. Between two deaths and two missing pets—not to mention a fire at the cabin Janine's husband had just finished—it hadn't turned out the way anyone had hoped. "I'm sorry to hear that. Is Philip still not feeling well because of his allergies?"

"Oh, he's much better now. That hot-water bottle did the trick, although the housekeepers must have taken it away because it's not in our room anymore."

Faith frowned. That didn't sound like something the housekeepers would do. They would have left something like that alone until the guest said he or she didn't need it anymore. Perhaps they'd simply put it away in a drawer and Philip and Janine hadn't found it yet. "Would you like me to speak to housekeeping about it? Do you need it back?"

Janine shook her head. "That's all right. I'll go to the front desk for another one if Philip's allergies flare up again."

"Do you want to tell me what's upsetting you? I get the feeling that's not it."

Janine gave her a small smile. "No, I'm not upset about a hot-water bottle. But if you have some work you need to do, I don't want to intrude."

Faith led her to the sitting area by the fireplace. She took one chair and patted the one beside her. "My primary duty here is helping our guests. Please come talk to me."

"Thank you." Janine perched on the edge of the chair. "Do you remember how I mentioned that Philip and I haven't had much time together lately?"

"Yes. You said the retreat was an ideal way to mix business with pleasure." Faith had hoped the couple's stay at the manor would bring them closer together. Even though Faith was never the one to suggest romance novels for the book club—that was Brooke's department—she was a bit of a romantic. She hated to see a strain in anyone's relationship.

"I thought we'd be able to spend some quality time together," Janine continued. "Both of us had interests here. And considering everything else, the timing was perfect."

"What do you mean, 'everything else'?" Faith asked.

"Oh, didn't I tell you?" Janine asked. "We had a fire at our home only a few days before we were scheduled to come here."

Faith gasped. "That's terrible. I hope no one was hurt."

"No, we were both away from the house at the time," Janine responded. "Fortunately, a neighbor noticed the flames and called the fire department."

"How bad was the damage?"

"We were very lucky. The house wasn't destroyed. Most of the damage came from smoke and the water used to douse the flames."

"So the trip to the manor gave you somewhere to stay while your house is being repaired?" Faith said.

"Exactly. We can't live in the house until it's professionally cleaned. A cleaning service is handling it now while we're away."

"The fire at the log cabin yesterday must have brought back some unpleasant memories," Faith said. It had been an awful sight for her, and her house hadn't nearly burned down less than a week before. She couldn't imagine how distressing it had been for Janine and Philip after what they'd gone through.

"It definitely did. And I'm afraid the two deaths may have reminded Philip of the loss of his parents. Death is always hard, but he seems to struggle with it more than anyone else I know."

"I'm very sorry," Faith said, resting a hand on the woman's arm. "I wish there was something I could do to help."

"I don't think there is unless you have a cure for recurring nightmares," Janine said. "Or for a magician's assistant who likes to drop juggling pins in the hallway."

"What do you mean?"

"Cody was practicing his juggling act right outside our room."

Faith couldn't believe that Cody would do something so inconsiderate. "Do you want me to talk to him? We don't want our guests disturbed, even by other guests."

"No, it's fine," Janine replied. "We asked him to move on, and he did."

"Did Cody mention why he was practicing in the hallway?"

"He said he was working on his control by practicing in areas with different heights and widths. Apparently, he's learning to study his environment so he knows how to adjust his performance to fit it."

It sounded like a logical reason. However, Faith knew that Cody's suite was down the hall from Janine and Philip's. She found it curious that Cody had been practicing outside their room instead of his own.

"By the way, Philip suspects Cody of taking the hot-water bottle."

"Why does he suspect Cody?" Faith asked.

"Philip noticed the hot-water bottle was gone shortly after Cody was practicing by our room," Janine explained. "The bottle was on a stand right inside the door so we'd remember to return it. Philip insists that Cody swiped it while we were asking him to practice somewhere else."

"How could Cody take it while you were watching him?"

"That's what I thought, but Philip reminded me that Cody's training with Fiona and she's teaching him sleight-of-hand skills. Of course, tricks like that are what make magicians successful. But I still don't see how he could have done it or why he'd take a hot-water bottle of all things. I keep telling Philip it must have been the housekeepers."

Faith frowned. "It is odd."

"Philip and I are both a little jumpy right now," Janine said. "I'm trying to convince myself that there's no reason to think that the fire at the cabin had anything to do with us. I mean, why would it? But at the same time, a fire at home and then a fire at our retreat? I can't truly believe that's a coincidence."

Faith wondered if Janine was right to be concerned. Could someone have been targeting Philip and Janine at their home? When the fire there hadn't succeeded, had the arsonist followed them to the manor in order to make another attempt on their lives?

Even if both fires had been deliberately set, had the arsonist planned to harm the couple, but the judge had been in the cabin instead?

In fact, any of the writers retreat attendees could have been in the cabin when it had been set on fire. Any one of them could have been the intended victim. And the judge certainly seemed to have been targeted, since his nurse had been murdered just before he was. But were the deaths and the fires related?

Faith wished she could find the answers to those questions, but she simply had no idea where to begin. After all, no one was going to admit to having tried to burn down the log cabin. It would be even more difficult to search for a perpetrator since she didn't know for sure that either fire was anything more than an accident.

And the mysterious fires didn't explain Diana's death.

"Was the fire marshal able to determine the cause of the fire at your home?" Faith asked.

"He was able to tell right away," Janine said. "Someone broke a window and let themselves in. According to the investigators, there was absolutely no doubt. It was arson."

The cat streaked down the hall, his sensitive nose leading him toward an unusual and enticing scent. He followed the smell until it led him to the large room with many tables.

The scent grew stronger and stronger as he slipped under one of the tables and saw an unfamiliar object stuck under a chair. He had located the source.

Creeping along with his belly pressed low to the floor, he advanced toward the strange sight before him.

A small creature with a pink nose and a swirl of fur on its head sat inside the clear, round object.

The cat crept closer, expecting the pathetic creature to run from him as quickly as its short legs could go.

The thing spotted him, and its nose twitched in the air. It moved its small feet, but it went nowhere.

The cat sidled right up next to the animal and stealthily extended a front paw. It was not a mouse or a rat. It seemed to be trapped inside the ball. He tapped on the side, but the object did not move. The cat bumped the ball with his nose, then pressed against it with his front paw once more.

The small furry creature inside stared at him as if begging for help.

How could the cat refuse? He couldn't imagine anything worse than confinement. He pushed and prodded until the clear ball broke free from where it was wedged beneath the chair.

The ball began to move as the thing ran inside it.

The cat followed the ball, giving it occasional nudges with his paw until he had guided it out the door of the large room and into the hallway. Using his paws and his nose, he directed the animal all the way back to the room containing his human. He was confident she would feel better if he brought her this tribute.

Inside the ball, the creature became excited and ran faster.

The cat chased it as it rolled past his human. He swept out a paw and tapped it once more.

The ball rolled into a small wooden stand near his human's desk. The stand shook from the force of the ball striking it, and it wobbled on its base.

Papers cascaded from the top of the stand and fluttered down around the cat and the ball.

His human hurried over and collected the pieces of paper, sticking an envelope in her pocket. When she spotted the ball, she beamed.

The cat sat down, ready to be praised for solving one of his person's problems.

Even though Faith had not wanted Watson to leave the cottage and had been worried ever since he dashed out of sight, she was grateful that he had located Prunella. She picked him up and cuddled him.

Watson purred and snuggled against her.

"You are one special cat. Thank you, Rumpy."

He stared at her, apparently offended that she'd used his nickname, then jumped down from her arms and turned his back on her.

Faith's laugh turned into a yawn. Her lack of sleep was catching up with her.

She scooped up the ball and examined Prunella. Faith was no guinea pig expert, but the animal appeared unharmed. She still didn't know who had killed Diana or the judge, but at least one mystery had a happy ending. "Let's get you back to Christina right away."

Faith tucked the guinea pig's ball under her arm and walked to the front desk to find out which suite Christina was staying in. She tried to walk as smoothly as possible, not wanting to cause any additional stress to the small creature.

She could only assume that Prunella had been on quite an adventure. She had no idea where Watson had found her, but it hardly mattered. The guinea pig was safe and sound.

Faith was going to enjoy seeing the delight on Christina's face when she was reunited with her beloved pet. She would also be pleased to inform Christina that Watson had been the one to find Prunella and return her safely. She hadn't appreciated Christina's suspicions about Watson's trustworthiness.

A young woman named Cara was manning the front desk when

Faith arrived. "Is that the misplaced guinea pig?" she asked, motioning to Prunella.

Christina must have stopped by the front desk to inquire about her pet.

Faith nodded, then briefly explained how she had come by the guinea pig. "Watson appeared inordinately pleased with himself when he careened into the library, batting Prunella's exercise ball ahead of him."

Cara laughed. "I wish I could have seen that."

"I'd like to return Prunella to Christina right away. Which suite is she staying in?"

"I saw her husband drop her off at the spa to get a facial," Cara replied. "She seemed very upset about Prunella, and I think he was trying to cheer her up."

After thanking Cara, Faith headed to the spa. "Don't worry," she murmured to the little creature on the way. "We'll get you back to your person soon."

Prunella burbled, and Faith hoped the sound was one of contentment.

Ina Garcia, one of the spa attendants, greeted Faith at the door and directed her to a treatment room in the back.

Faith wound her way through the opulent space, decorated in calming shades of dove gray, white, and robin's-egg blue. Soothing instrumental music played quietly through hidden speakers. Dainty herbal and floral aromas drifted past Faith's nose. The same care and attention to detail found in the rest of the property was apparent in the spa as well. No matter what was going on, it was impossible to step inside and not feel calmer and more grounded.

Christina wore a fluffy white robe, and she was relaxing in a plush chair with her feet in a porcelain bowl filled with steaming, sudsy water. Her face was encased in a thick green paste, and her eyes were covered by a cooling gel mask.

Faith approached Christina and softly called her name so as not to startle her.

Christina pulled the mask from her eyes and gasped with delight when she saw Prunella. She squealed and held out her arms.

As Faith handed the ball to her, she said, "I don't know anything about guinea pigs, but she appears to be fine."

"Where did you find her?" Christina pried open the ball and clutched her tiny friend to her chest.

The guinea pig made more of the burbling noises Faith had heard earlier.

"I didn't find her," Faith said. "Watson did. He ran off on his own and brought her back to the library. I can only assume she was trapped somewhere and he managed to free her."

"I'm so relieved she's safe," Christina said as she stroked the little animal's furry back. "I'm almost finished here, so I'll be able to get her some food and water. And I'm sorry I accused your cat. I was so upset that I wasn't being reasonable. Will you thank Watson for me?"

"I'll be sure to let him know that you appreciate his efforts," Faith replied, amused.

"Won't you stay and have a pedicure?" Christina asked. "It would be my treat to make up for accusing Watson of taking Prunella."

"Thank you for the offer, but it really isn't necessary," Faith said. "Besides, I'm afraid I have to get back to my responsibilities in the library."

"Well, thank you again. Let me know if you change your mind," Christina said before turning her full attention to the little creature seated in her lap.

As Faith hurried back to the library, she remembered the envelope that had fallen off the small stand when Watson had knocked Prunella's ball into its narrow base. She reached into her pocket and pulled it out. Her name was written clearly across the front of it. She didn't recognize the handwriting, but it was not unusual for guests and staff alike to leave messages for Faith at the library.

Faith turned the envelope over and noticed that the flap was sealed. She slipped her finger beneath the flap and carefully eased it open. When she removed a folded piece of paper from the envelope, she recognized the stationery as the kind provided in the guest suites. She felt a cold wave of fear wash over her as she read the message.

Dear Faith,

I am leaving this note in the library where I am quite certain Judge Davidson will never think to look for it. As I'm sure you've noticed, the judge is not an avid reader, so it's unlikely he'll spend much time in the library.

You must wonder what I want to say to you that I would not wish for my employer to see. While I still hold out hope that the judge will do the right thing, I am afraid that my life may be in danger. Should anything happen to me while I am at Castleton Manor, I trust that you will share this note with the police.

As you know, Judge Davidson required surgery not long before the retreat. I felt it my duty to be in the recovery room when he awakened. It's common for patients to have vivid dreams and utter bizarre statements as they are coming out from under anesthesia. This was the case, or at least I thought it was, with the judge after his surgery.

As he was recovering consciousness, Judge Davidson rambled nonstop about payoffs and bribes concerning cases that had come before his bench throughout his long career. I thought nothing of it at the time, and I soon forgot all about it.

Until we arrived at the manor.

It seemed that much of what I had considered ramblings brought on by anesthesia had a ring of truth to it. Several of the other guests mentioned the judge's poor character and their suspicions that he had acted improperly in their cases. I could not put their accusations out of my mind, so I took my concerns to the judge.

I told him what he had said in the recovery room, and I urged him to go to the authorities and confess what he had done. I said that I suspected much of the trouble with his heart had to do with the weight of his conscience.

He promised he would confess, but he begged me to allow him to finish the retreat before he did it.

I agreed to wait, but I soon regretted my decision. While he continued to treat me as he always had, I have caught him looking at me with sheer loathing more and more. I am quite nervous about his intentions, and while I won't go back on my word, I felt it would be wise to take steps to expose him should I come to harm.

By leaving this letter with you, I have also provided a way to ensure that the authorities will know what the judge has done if he chooses to renege on his agreement to confess to his crimes. He must be held to account no matter what.

I have always found a library to be a tremendous resource and a place where truth is valued. I'm counting on you, Faith, to make sure that continues to be the case.

Sincerest regards,

Diana Marsden

Faith stared at the note in her hand. She hated to believe that it was possible, but it seemed that all the rumors bandied about concerning the judge were likely true.

Faith had wondered if the snake had killed Diana. But Diana's note made it seem much more likely that Gunther, wherever he was, could not be blamed for Diana's death. If Diana's note was to be believed, there was every reason to assume that the judge had murdered her.

Faith called the police immediately. Fortunately, Chief Garris was available. As soon as she told him about the note, he said he'd be right over.

Then Faith ran downstairs to Marlene's office and rapped on the door.

"Come in," Marlene called.

Faith burst into the office and shut the door behind her, leaning against it to catch her breath.

Marlene sat behind her large desk. She appeared as polished and put together as always. Her blonde hair was impeccably coiffed, and not a speck of lint marred the lapels of her navy-blue suit jacket.

While Marlene looked well turned out, she did not seem pleased to see Faith. She drummed her freshly manicured fingernails on the surface of her polished wooden desk and let out an exaggerated sigh. "Is there something you need?"

Faith thrust out the envelope and waved it in front of the assistant manager. "I found this in the library this morning. It had been left on a stand under a stack of other paperwork that I hadn't gone through yet."

"Why would I be interested in reading your private correspondence?" Marlene asked, eyeing the letter in Faith's outstretched hand with apparent distaste. "It isn't a love note from our employer, is it? Being forced to watch the two of you wandering around the manor all starry-eyed is bad enough."

Faith felt as though she might lose her temper. She silently counted to three, then ten, and reminded herself that a confrontation with Marlene would only slow down the investigation. Faith needed to solve the mystery much more than she needed to argue with her supervisor.

"It's not from Wolfe, and you will want to read it because it helps to explain why at least one of our guests has turned up dead," Faith said, careful to keep her tone even.

Marlene sprang to her feet and snatched the envelope from Faith's hand. She yanked out the note and unfolded it so quickly Faith worried she would tear it. Marlene's eyes widened as she read.

"I've already called the chief," Faith said. "He's on his way."

Marlene nodded. "I'll keep the note. Go back to the library, and don't tell anyone else about the note. It might be the first break the chief has had in the case."

Faith understood what she wasn't saying. *We don't want to let a killer know we might be on the track that leads us to him or her.*

18

Chief Garris stood in the doorway to the library in less than half an hour. Faith thought he looked as tired as she felt, but he smiled at her as warmly as ever.

Garris crossed the room in a few long strides and took a seat before the fireplace next to Faith. He opened a file folder and removed a plastic bag holding the envelope containing Diana's letter. "Ms. Russell gave me the note. I think you've given us a great deal of help in clearing up what happened to Ms. Marsden. How did you find it?"

"It was Watson who found it," Faith said.

Watson was sitting on Faith's lap, and he glanced up at her with a smug expression.

As she told the chief her story, it seemed all the more remarkable that Watson had once again helped get to the heart of a mystery. If it weren't for him, that letter could have stayed hidden beneath other bits of stray paper even longer than it had. Perhaps long enough to send the murder investigation in the wrong direction.

"Good work, Watson," the chief said as he scratched the cat's chin. "As soon as I have a chance, I'll stop by Happy Tails and pick you up a box of tunaroons as a thank-you gift."

Watson meowed.

Faith smiled. "I think that means he appreciates it, though I don't think it's necessary."

Watson glared at her, his stubbed tail twitching in irritation. As far as he was concerned, tunaroons were always necessary.

"I had just finished reading the autopsy report when you called the station," Garris said.

"Was the judge responsible for Diana's death?"

"It seems there's no doubt that Ms. Marsden was deliberately strangled by a human, though we haven't found the murder weapon yet. According to the description Ms. Perkins gave of Gunther, it appeared that the ligature used to strangle her was narrower than the snake is. While Gunther may still pose a threat, he is off the suspect list for Ms. Marsden's murder."

Faith momentarily felt a wave of relief wash over her that Gunther hadn't killed Diana. Until she thought of the judge. Although it seemed likely he had murdered his nurse, she doubted very much that he had killed himself, particularly in the exact same way he had killed Diana. Could Gunther still pose a threat? Or had another of the human guests been responsible for Judge Davidson's death?

"Even if the judge was responsible for Diana's murder, it doesn't explain how he died, does it?" Faith said.

"I'm afraid not." The chief slid the note back into his file folder before getting to his feet.

"Do you know what killed him?" Faith asked.

"Not yet, but I'm willing to bet there's still a murderer on the loose who is responsible for at least Judge Davidson's death, if not both."

Faith spent the rest of the day assisting patrons and catching up on paperwork in the library.

She was relieved when it was time to go home and get ready for the book club meeting. With all the horrible events of the past few days, Faith was more eager than ever to spend some time with her friends. She was especially looking forward to seeing Midge, who was back from her trip, and asking her advice about the missing python.

As Faith crossed the Great Hall Gallery with Watson trotting at her side, she saw Cody juggling again.

Cody stopped when he noticed Faith. "Have you heard anything about Gunther?"

"Unfortunately, no," she answered, not wanting to admit that finding the snake had fallen pretty far down her list of priorities, what with two murders and a fire at the cabin. "I'm meeting my veterinarian friend later, and I hope she'll be able to help us with the search."

"I hope so too." Cody checked his watch. "I'd better go. I need to get ready for dinner."

As Cody stuffed his juggling pins into a large duffel bag, Watson scampered over and peeked inside.

Faith didn't want Watson to mess with Cody's belongings, so she went to pick him up.

Watson squirmed out of her grasp and pawed at something tucked into the corner of the bag.

"I'm sorry," Faith told Cody. "I don't know what's gotten into him."

Cody picked up the object that had claimed Watson's interest. It was a hot-water bottle. "What's this doing in here? It's not mine."

Had Cody stolen it from Janine and Philip's room after all? Faith studied Cody's expression. Was he genuinely surprised to see the bottle? If so, she couldn't help but wonder how he hadn't noticed it in his bag before. Or was he pretending to be surprised?

Without another word, Cody tossed the bottle into the duffel, slung it over his shoulder, and rushed away.

Faith and Watson left the manor, and Watson raced ahead of her on the path.

While she followed him home, she considered what she'd seen. Why would Cody break into Janine and Philip's room and take a hot-water bottle they'd borrowed from the manor? She shook her head. It didn't make any sense. But it didn't change the fact that Watson had found it in Cody's duffel bag. What was it doing in there?

When they entered the cottage, Watson made a beeline for the kitchen.

"And people say cats are mysterious and hard to read," she said, laughing.

Faith filled Watson's food and water bowls, then had leftover tortellini with a classic red sauce and a glass of iced tea.

Wolfe called while she was tidying up the kitchen. She filled him in on Diana's letter and her conversation with the chief. She also told him about Watson's discovery of the lost guinea pig.

"I'm glad Watson is there to help you. And I know I say this a lot, but please be careful," Wolfe told her. "I worry about you, especially since these things have a way of becoming dangerous when you poke into them."

"I think it became dangerous when a ten-foot python escaped from his terrarium," Faith replied. "But don't worry. Watson keeps an eye on me. You just focus on your business trip and coming back safe." She checked the kitchen clock. "I'm sorry, but I need to run. It's the book club meeting tonight."

"I hope they're keeping you out of trouble too."

Faith laughed. "Have you met them? You know full well that every single one of those women is more likely to get me into trouble than keep me out of it."

"That's true, but a guy can hope," he teased.

After agreeing that they would need to have a date when he got back, they hung up.

Faith grabbed her purse and headed to the door. "Do you want to go to town?" she asked her cat.

Watson jumped down from his perch on the couch and beat her to the door.

The sun was starting to sink in the sky when Faith and Watson arrived at the Candle House Library in Lighthouse Bay. As the name suggested, it had once been used to manufacture candles. The three-story stone building was charming, and it still housed much of the original glass in the windows. The interior had been modernized and updated to house the library, but the entire building retained its character. Every time she visited it, Faith thought how fortunate the town was that the old candle house had been preserved and transformed into such a lovely privately funded library.

Faith opened the door and stepped across the threshold, Watson at her heels. She glanced up at the massive wooden beams that spanned the ceiling as she headed for the book club's favorite gathering spot.

Comfy reading chairs surrounded the impressive fireplace, where the candlemakers had processed the tallow used in their craft. However, there was no need for a fire this evening as the weather was pleasant and mild.

Faith was delighted to see that the rest of the book club members were already assembled with their books in their laps.

They greeted Faith and Watson with bright smiles.

Eileen was the leader of the group. Faith and her aunt had always been close, and the fact that she lived in Lighthouse Bay was one of the reasons Faith had been so eager to accept the position at the manor.

Brooke sat to Eileen's right. She'd changed from her chef's coat into a flowy sundress with a bold floral pattern. Her necklace and earrings added to it without being overwhelming—a balance Faith felt she never handled quite as well. Brooke's penchant for fashion was a point of interest for the rest of her friends.

Unlike Midge and Faith, Brooke didn't bring her pets to the meetings. Although she would have been more than welcome to, she always protested that the angelfish, Diva and Bling, would find the trip too stressful, not to mention possibly messy. Her friends knew that this meant Brooke actually felt that way, but they didn't challenge her deeply held belief that her fish communicated their feelings to her, including when "they" thought she was dating a loser.

Faith was relieved to see that Midge had indeed returned to town in time to join them for their meeting, sporting her trademark fuchsia lipstick and freshly manicured nails, which featured a flower made of paw prints on each thumb.

Her Chihuahua, Atticus, was perched on her lap. Midge and her husband, Peter, were empty nesters, and she had a habit of doting on Atticus to handle the situation, often by dressing him up. This evening was no exception. He sported a tiny leather jacket with a patch on the back emblazoned with the words *Born to Be Mild*.

Faith stifled a chuckle as she noticed Atticus trying to pull off his expensive Doggles. Midge had diagnosed her dog with vision problems and had made the decision to have him fitted with a prescription pair of eyewear designed to correct the difficulty.

Atticus had not taken to the glasses with enthusiasm. In fact, more often than not he could be seen shaking his head and trying to pry them off with a paw. Unluckily for him, Midge was thoroughly devoted to his health and managed to keep them firmly in place most of the time.

Faith wondered if Watson would ever grow to think of Atticus as more than a nuisance, but she doubted it. He made no effort to hide his disdain for the tiny dog when he entered the room with Faith, turning up his nose when Atticus wagged his tail hopefully. When Faith sat in the remaining empty chair, Watson hopped up into her lap, turned around three times, and deliberately turned his back on Atticus.

"How was your vacation?" Faith asked Midge in an effort to smooth over Watson's rudeness. "Was it as much fun as you hoped it would be?"

"Even more," Midge said. "If you ever get the chance to take a train tour out west, I highly recommend it."

"Midge was just telling us about it before you arrived," Eileen said. "It sounded like quite an adventure."

"I hear you've been having adventures—or maybe misadventures—of your own while I've been gone," Midge said. "What have I missed?"

Eileen and Brooke turned to Faith and gave her a pointed look as if to say she should tell the story.

Faith cleared her throat and rested a hand on Watson's back to center herself as she recalled the harrowing events of the past few days. Surrounded by her friends' encouraging and supportive faces, she felt some of her anxiety seep away.

"Do you remember how excited I was about the log cabin and the retreat for memoir writers this week?" Faith asked.

"Of course I do," Midge answered. "I was really sorry that my vacation coincided with the scheduled completion of the cabin. I had hoped to see it right away."

"I think you're lucky to have missed its grand opening," Faith said.

"Oh dear," Midge said. "What happened?"

"We've had one and possibly two murders, arson at the log cabin, and a missing guinea pig and reticulated python," Faith said all in a rush.

Midge raised her eyebrows in surprise.

Even Atticus sat up and stared at Faith through his thick Doggles.

"I've obviously missed a great deal," Midge remarked. "Who died?"

"Two of the retreat guests."

"And they were closely connected, weren't they?" Eileen asked.

"Yes, they were," Faith said. "The death the police have determined was murder was that of Diana Marsden, a private nurse. The second death was that of her patient, Judge Jerome Davidson."

"Judge Davidson," Midge said thoughtfully. "Why do I know that name?"

"He presided over several high-profile cases," Faith replied. "Maybe you read about him in the newspaper at some point."

"I seem to remember an accident in the entertainment industry with a surprise ruling," Midge said. "Something with a magician, I think."

"That was The Fantastical Fiona lawsuit," Faith said. "Despite overwhelming evidence supporting her, the judge ruled in favor of the defendant."

"Such a tragedy," Eileen said. She turned to Faith. "I really enjoyed her show that we went to together in Boston. Do you remember?"

"How could I forget? It was quite an evening."

"She wears the most amazing outfits even when she's not onstage," Brooke said enthusiastically. "She makes a veil and gloves look so chic."

"That was the case I was thinking of," Midge said. "Is she at the manor this week too, by any chance?"

"Yes, along with her assistant and her reticulated python, Gunther," Faith said.

"Is that the snake that's lost?" Midge asked.

"Yes," Faith said. "It appears that someone let him out of his terrarium, and he hasn't been seen since."

"How long has it been since anyone has seen him?" Midge asked.

"A few days," Faith said. "I don't mind telling you it's been quite upsetting, especially with all the other things that have gone wrong this week."

Brooke nodded, sending her dangling earrings swinging. "I've been jumpy ever since I heard there was a snake on the loose. Even if it had been a small one I would've been upset, but one the size of Gunther is really scary."

"How large is Gunther?" Midge asked, leaning forward.

"At least ten feet long," Faith said.

"I don't think I could have easily wrapped both hands around him," Brooke said, holding up her hands to demonstrate.

"I assume you've scoured the manor looking for him?" Midge said.

Faith shivered. The conversation was rekindling all her worry and tension over the python. "We've searched, and we called in animal control while you were away. But no one has seen Gunther. As far as I know, they haven't found a single clue pointing to where he is or where he's been. And Fiona is eager to get him back."

"She should be," Midge said. "Even if her python doesn't hurt anyone, I expect that he could be in danger."

Faith had not given much consideration to Gunther's well-being. She had thought about how the cool evening temperatures might affect him, and she had briefly considered the possibility that Athena could have wounded him if he had attacked Diana. She felt a little guilty that she had not considered his safety more. If the missing pet had been cuddly and furry like Watson or even Prunella, she knew she would have felt more concerned.

"Do you think Gunther is in danger?" Eileen asked.

"At the very least, a reticulated python—or any reptile for that matter—needs to find a way to maintain its body temperature," Midge explained. "I expect that he will be found somewhere doing precisely that."

"You said 'at the very least,'" Faith responded. "What else does he need to survive?"

"When was the last time Gunther ate?" Midge asked.

"I can tell you he hasn't stopped by the kitchen for a snack," Brooke said with a shudder.

"I really don't know," Faith said. "When Fiona arrived, she and her assistant were talking about feeding him. But he disappeared the next day. I assume he had his regular feeding schedule until then."

"Do you think that's important?" Eileen asked.

"Even though snakes don't feed every day or even every other day, it might be important," Midge said. "I'll come by in the morning and see if I can spot anything that animal control missed."

Gratitude and relief washed over Faith. If anyone could find the snake, it was Midge. "Thank you."

"The only thing that I absolutely advise you to do is to keep an eye on Watson," Midge continued. "With a snake that size, there's no telling the harm he could do to other creatures. Especially considering that he's probably hungry."

19

Before going to work the next morning, Faith called Marlene to ask if Gunther had been found during the night.

When Marlene reported that the snake was still unaccounted for, Faith called Midge at the pet bakery. Her friend picked up on the first ring, and Faith relayed the information—or more accurately, the lack of information.

"Let me give some instructions to my staff, and I'll be over as soon as I can," Midge said.

Faith placed her breakfast dishes in the sink and leaned against the counter to steady her nerves for the search ahead. She had felt uncomfortable enough conducting a search when Gunther had first vanished. That was before he'd had time to become desperately hungry. Did ten-foot snakes ever get ravenous enough to attempt to eat humans?

Unfortunately, there was nothing else to be done. If she ever wanted things to get back to normal at the manor, the snake would have to be found. Surely an expert like Midge, who had experience with exotic reptiles, would have some idea of where to locate him. She suspected Roland from animal control wouldn't mind turning the search over to Midge. No one could really enjoy looking for a large reptile.

Faith found Watson sleeping on the back of the sofa in the living room. When she lifted her purse from a nearby chair, the cat opened his eyes, jumped to the floor, and ran to the door.

She picked him up and held him tightly to her chest. "You can only come with me if you promise to stay where I can keep an eye on you all day. No escaping and no running off to explore on your own. Do you understand me, mister?"

Watson stared at her, then slowly blinked as if to say he had received her message loud and clear.

Sometimes she wondered how much he actually comprehended. It was as though he understood everything she said to him and many things she didn't say.

Faith carefully locked the door behind her and intended to do the same when she got to the library. Anyone who needed to come in could knock. If Midge was able to flush out Gunther, Faith wasn't taking any chances with her cat.

She carried Watson to the manor and into the library. To her surprise, he didn't even struggle to be put down.

Midge arrived a few minutes later.

"Thanks again for coming," Faith said. "I don't know what I'd do without you."

"Don't mention it," Midge said. "I'm always happy to help."

Watson twined around Midge's ankles and purred.

Smiling, Midge reached into her tote and took out a small bag. "I know you're just buttering me up for one of these." She gave Watson a tunaroon.

The cat sat down to enjoy his treat.

"I've spoken to Marlene, and she's going to tell Roland I'm taking over," Midge said. "And she's putting Laura in charge of the library today, so you're free to join me."

"Lucky me," Faith muttered.

While they waited for Laura to arrive, they searched every square inch of the library to no avail.

Laura strode into the room with a backpack slung over her shoulder and smiled. "Good morning."

"Thanks for taking over for me today," Faith said.

"It's my pleasure. I'd rather be doing this than what you'll be doing any day." Laura set her backpack down on the table and removed a textbook, a pencil, and a notebook. "I'm hoping to get some homework done."

"Good luck," Faith said. "The library should be fairly quiet. There are a lot of workshops scheduled. But call or text me if you need anything. And please make sure Watson stays in here with you if you can."

"I'll try," Laura promised.

Faith and Midge left Laura and Watson in the library and began their hunt for Gunther.

"Let's stick together," Midge suggested. "As they say, two heads are better than one."

Faith was relieved that they were going to search in tandem. The only thing that sounded worse than looking for a huge, probably ravenous python was doing so alone.

Faith and Midge methodically searched the rooms on the first floor of the manor. They poked through the greenery in the conservatory and examined both spas—the one for people and the one for pets. Then they went downstairs to the basement and checked the kitchen, the laundry room, and the offices.

Nothing.

Midge crossed her arms over her chest. "Marlene says that Roland checked the third floor and that no one has been up there since, not even housekeeping, and the doors have been kept locked since none of the Jaxons are here right now." The third floor was Wolfe and his family's residence when they were in town, and guests weren't permitted to go up there. "I don't think we need to look there or in the second-floor suites either. If Gunther was in anyone's room, you would have heard about it."

Faith nodded.

"Did anyone check the tunnels?" Midge asked.

"Philip Peters, the architect who designed the log cabin, searched them the first day. He didn't find any evidence of Gunther."

"I'm not surprised," Midge said decisively. "Gunther is cold-blooded. He would seek out warm places, not the cooler temperatures below the manor. On the other hand, if he did make his way down there, he won't be feeling very frisky. The cold makes reptiles somewhat lethargic."

Faith had not considered that the chill in the tunnels could be an advantage. But the idea of being underground with a giant snake filled her with dread no matter how lethargic Gunther might be.

"Let's explore the tunnels," Midge said. She removed two flashlights from her tote bag and handed one to Faith. "I don't know if we'll need these, but I'd rather be prepared."

Faith and Midge headed down the corridor. As they turned a corner, they saw Watson sitting in the middle of the hallway, as if he'd been waiting for them.

"I told you to stay in the library," Faith chided him. "How did you sneak out? Laura must be frantic."

Watson didn't respond. Instead, he nonchalantly washed his face while Faith texted Laura to let her know they'd found him.

Thank goodness, she replied. *I took my eyes off him for two minutes and he was gone.*

Midge laughed. "Apparently, he didn't want to be left out of the search party. He'll be faster than Gunther in the tunnels, so I'm sure it'll be fine if he joins us. But he should stay close just in case."

Faith still didn't feel entirely comfortable about letting Watson roam the tunnels, but she knew she couldn't stop him. He definitely had a mind of his own. Besides, her cat was intelligent and resourceful, and he had proven time and again that he could take good care of himself. She texted Laura to let her know Watson would be staying with them.

They walked to a door at the far end of a long hallway on the first floor. Faith flicked on the light at the top of a narrow stairwell. A bare bulb hung from the ceiling and cast a miserly amount of light on the steep stairs. This seldom-used stairwell was the opposite of the one to the basement, which was pleasant and brightly lit.

Faith took a deep breath, then aimed her flashlight into the void below.

Watson rubbed against her ankles, making a sound somewhere between a short meow and a purr. Then he trotted down the stairs.

Encouraged by his bravery, Faith slowly began her own descent. She was more than a little grateful for the sound of Midge's feet tapping on the stairs behind her.

Every few steps, Watson paused and glanced back at her, meowing gently as if coaxing her down the stairs.

Despite her mounting fear, Faith pressed ahead.

At the bottom of the stairs, the tunnels branched out in two directions.

"Right or left?" Faith asked Midge.

Watson headed to the right without hesitation.

"Watson seems to think we should go that way," Midge said, pointing her flashlight beam to the side he had indicated.

Faith's heart sank. She avoided coming down here, but she knew there were small, dungeon-like rooms in that direction.

Suddenly Watson's easy trot became a dash. Her pet glanced back over his shoulder as if to urge her forward.

Faith hurried after him. She wished that he would slow down. How could she make a thorough search for the snake if she was walking so fast? After all, there were branches of tunnels leading away from the main corridor at frequent intervals. Gunther could be hiding in any one of them.

When they entered one of the small rooms, Watson stopped abruptly—so abruptly that Faith almost tripped over him. He batted at something in front of him.

Faith trained her flashlight beam on Watson and the object of his interest.

"What's a cooler doing here?" Midge asked as she joined them.

"I don't know." Faith studied the cooler. It was large and red, with a white top. On one end was a handle. It had a set of wheels on the side closest to Watson and appeared to be brand-new, as a price sticker from a local store was still attached to it.

As Faith ran the beam of her flashlight over the surface of the cooler, she noticed a peculiar set of random holes drilled into the side. There were no identifying marks on it, and she couldn't imagine why something like that would be abandoned in the tunnels.

Unless it hadn't been abandoned but left down here deliberately.

Faith bent over the cooler and placed her hand on the lid, unease roiling in her belly.

Watson gave a warning yowl.

Midge stood next to Faith and rested a hand on her friend's arm. "I think we need to open it, but let's be careful." She trained her flashlight beam directly on the cooler lid, then nodded.

Faith took a deep breath, unlatched the lid, and slowly opened it. Midge's flashlight beam illuminated the contents, and Faith felt as though she had been punched in the stomach.

There, coiled and taking up most of the space inside the cooler, lay the missing python. He was wrapped around a hot-water bottle.

Faith held her breath as Midge bent forward and carefully reached for the hot-water bottle. She pressed the back of her hand against it as if taking its temperature, then removed her hand slowly and motioned for Faith to lower the lid.

"The water bottle is lukewarm," Midge said. "Someone has obviously been taking care of the snake, and I would expect that whoever it is will return soon in order to reheat the bottle."

Cody. Janine had said Cody had been right outside their room and that Philip noticed the hot-water bottle had disappeared soon after. Watson had found a hot-water bottle in the young man's duffel bag. Cody was learning tricks of illusion and escape from Fiona. Did those skills also include breaking and entering? It seemed like a lot of trouble to go to for a hot-water bottle, especially since he could have simply asked for one. And why would he hide Gunther from his own employer? It didn't make any sense.

"We'd better contact the police," Faith said. "It must have

something to do with the deaths of Diana and the judge. I just don't know what yet."

"Good idea." Midge pulled her cell phone from her pocket. "I don't have a signal. Do you?"

Faith checked her phone. "No."

"Let's go upstairs and call the police," Midge suggested.

"If the person coming to reheat the hot-water bottle arrives before the police, we won't know who it is unless one of us remains behind to keep watch," Faith said. "You go make the call."

"We could stand by the door upstairs to make the call. That way, the person would have to walk right by us to get down here."

Faith shook her head. "We don't know the layout of these tunnels. There could be other ways in from different parts of the manor, even from outside. One of us needs to go call the police, and one of us has to stay here in case whoever took Gunther comes back in the meantime."

"You go," Midge said.

"You should go. You'll be able to give an account of Gunther's health, at least at a glance. And if the police want Fiona to come down with them, you can recommend things for her to bring for him."

"Are you sure?" Midge said.

"I'll be fine," Faith said. "You go, and take Watson with you."

Midge picked up the cat. "I'll be back as soon as I can."

Faith nodded and waved her friend off. She watched as Midge hurried out of sight. As her friend's flashlight beam disappeared from view, Faith felt her courage begin to fade too.

She needed to wait out of plain sight, so she scanned the area for a place to hide. Beyond the cooler, another tunnel branched off from the room. Faith rushed over to the dark space. With reluctance, she switched off her flashlight and pulled her cell phone from her pocket. Then she pressed the video button and left it open, ready to start filming.

She sent up a silent prayer that Chief Garris would appear before Cody did.

20

It felt like hours that Faith hid in the darkness, waiting for a kidnapper and potential killer, but it was only a few minutes according to the clock on her phone.

Suddenly, a noise sounded from somewhere far along one of the tunnels. It was difficult to tell where the noise was coming from because it bounced off the walls of the stone space in every direction.

Faith felt all the muscles in her body tighten.

A weak beam of light bobbed toward her from the opposite end of the tunnel where she and Midge had entered earlier. So there was another entrance.

She felt a stab of hope, thinking it might be Chief Garris and a couple of his police officers. But even with the strange echoing sound, she thought she heard only one set of footsteps.

As the sound of the newcomer grew louder, Faith knew she must act. She crept forward to the very edge of her hiding place and turned on the video recorder on her cell phone. She reached forward enough to frame the cooler in the viewfinder.

A figure approached.

Faith squinted in the darkness.

Philip Peters came into view.

Faith almost gasped. *Don't jump to conclusions. Maybe he's making another search for Gunther. And if he's not, well, I certainly don't want him to know I'm here.*

Philip aimed his flashlight at the cooler, apparently not at all surprised to see it there. He bent down and placed a large thermos on the floor, then gingerly lifted the lid and pointed his flashlight beam inside the cooler. He reached inside with his free hand and removed the hot-water bottle.

Her heart sank. No. Philip's been keeping the snake down here. But why?

Faith kept filming his actions as he closed the cooler and emptied the hot-water bottle, pouring the old water out. The sound of the water splashing onto the stone floor echoed eerily through the confined space.

When the bottle was empty, he poured steaming hot water from the thermos into the bottle and replaced the cap with a firm twist. He raised the lid of the cooler once more.

Faith instinctively took a step back, and her foot scraped loudly against the stone. She froze.

Philip straightened. "Hello?"

She shrank back as far as she could while still keeping Philip within the range of her camera.

"Who's there?" Philip demanded.

Faith stayed put and held her breath.

Philip glared toward her hiding place. "I know you're there."

Faith knew there was nothing to do but emerge from her spot. If she didn't, he was sure to come and find her anyway. Still recording, she stepped out of the shadows. She held her cell phone down low and hoped he wouldn't notice it. "It's just me."

Philip trained the beam of his flashlight on her face.

She was momentarily blinded and at a distinct disadvantage. He could see her clearly, but she had difficulty keeping an eye on him. Or on the snake.

"What are you doing here?" Philip asked.

"I was searching for Gunther," Faith said.

"I guess you found him." His tone was even and cold, not his normally kind, friendly voice.

"Was he in the cooler when you helped me search the manor?" Faith asked. "Did you bring him down here?"

"Does it matter?"

"It does to me."

"Okay," Philip said. "I can't let you survive this, you know. I'll satisfy your last bit of curiosity, so you can see it's nothing personal."

Faith had plenty more curiosity, as well as a healthy dose of fear. Would Philip really kill her? He had the snake, but had he killed Diana and the judge? She steeled herself for his confession.

"Yes, I took him."

Faith willed her trembling hand to hold the camera steady and keep it focused on the man in front of her. She hoped that her cell phone was recording the entire conversation clearly. "Why would you do that?"

"Because the judge was frightened of snakes," Philip said.

"You took Fiona's snake to terrify the judge?" Faith asked. "What could you possibly have hoped to accomplish with that?"

"I thought seeing Gunther on the loose might give Judge Davidson a fatal heart attack," Philip said simply. "But I wasn't that lucky."

"You can't really mean that," Faith said. It occurred to her that she barely knew this man. She had no idea what he would or wouldn't do. He certainly didn't seem to feel bad for having wanted to frighten an old man, possibly to death. But she had to try to appeal to his better nature. "Think about what you're saying."

"That's exactly what I mean, but it doesn't seem to have worked out that way." Philip dropped his gaze to Faith's cell phone. He trained the beam of his flashlight on her hand, then back up at her face. "Are you recording this?"

"I had my phone out for extra light in case the flashlight died," Faith said. Even to her own ears her words sounded lame. Her hand started to shake even more violently. She glanced down to make sure Philip was still framed in her viewfinder.

"No matter. Once you're gone, your phone will disappear." Philip bent down and reached into the cooler, then lifted the python out of the cooler.

Her mouth dried as Gunther raised his head and flicked out his tongue as if searching the air.

Holding the snake out in front of him, Philip rushed over to Faith and snatched her phone before she could react. He tossed the phone to the floor and stomped on it with a sickening crunch.

He set the snake on the floor, then turned and ran toward the stairs, leaving Gunther in front of Faith, huge and writhing and blocking her only escape.

The cat didn't want to leave his human to fend for herself with the snake. But his human's friend grabbed him without so much as a by-your-leave, and she held him tightly as she rushed away.

He must do something to help his person. He twisted and squirmed but to no avail. He considered using his claws, but even though this was the person who gave him shots and investigated him quite boldly on a cold metal table every so often, she was also the one who made tunaroons. He didn't want to scratch her. He must wait for a window of opportunity.

It came when she reached the top of the stairs and put one of the humans' ever-present devices to her ear. As she spoke to someone he couldn't see, he felt her grip on him loosen gradually.

With a mighty wrench, he sprang from her embrace and sprinted back to his human.

When he got there, the reptile was advancing slowly toward his person. Honestly, he'd been gone for mere minutes and she was already in trouble. This was why he couldn't leave her alone.

His human seemed frozen in place, and the cat could smell her fear even across the room.

The cat leaped between his human and the enormous reptile and watched the animal move back and forth, creeping toward his human.

Every few inches it paused and raised its head. The cat knew it was attempting to smell his human with its tongue.

He arched his back and puffed out his fur in warning. The snake was much larger than others of its ilk he'd encountered, but he was determined to defend his person against any threat. Even one as big as this.

Especially one as big as this.

The reptile slithered even closer. It lifted its broad head far above the cat's own.

His human cried out behind him.

He knew she wished to protect him, but he couldn't stand by and do nothing while she was harmed.

The cat let loose a string of verbal warnings to the python. If it did not heed them, he would use force.

"Watson, no!" Faith watched in terror as Watson appeared out of nowhere and positioned himself directly between her and the enormous snake. She tried to grab her cat, but he danced out of her reach.

Watson arched his back into a menacing curve. He let out a series of yowls and hisses that were like nothing Faith had ever heard from him before.

But if she remembered correctly, snakes processed sound differently than humans did. She thought it likely that Watson's vocal defense would have less impact on the python than it would on other kinds of creatures.

Her heart pounded mercilessly in her chest, and she felt as though time had crawled to a stop. She knew that it had not been long since Midge had gone to get help, but it seemed like an eternity.

What had Philip hoped to accomplish by letting the snake loose? Had he expected her to die of fright as he had hoped the judge would do? Did he think that the snake would lash out at her and squeeze her until she suffocated before she could tell anyone what he had done?

Now that she thought about it, she wasn't sure that Midge had made it upstairs before Philip arrived. What if he had done something to keep her from calling the police? Was there anyone coming to help at all?

She fumbled in her pocket for her flashlight, pulled it out, and flipped it on. She pointed the beam of light directly in Gunther's face. Maybe he'd be disoriented by the sudden brightness.

She hoped that the quick change of light would not put Watson at a disadvantage. After all, a cat's eyesight was well adapted to the dark, and a flash of light might be confusing, even though she was shining it past him rather than at him.

But the flashlight didn't seem to affect the cat or the python.

Gunther slithered forward, finally coming within a flicking tongue's distance of Faith's beloved cat.

Watson gave a final hiss and raised his paw as if to strike the larger animal with it.

Suddenly, Faith heard the clattering of many pairs of feet on the stone floor. Flashlight beams bobbed in the hallway.

Disregarding Watson's protestations and the proximity of the enormous snake, Faith grabbed her cat and took several steps backward, all the while keeping the flashlight beam on Gunther.

"We're over here!" she called out. "The snake is loose."

She almost burst into tears of relief as Midge, Chief Garris, and Officer Jan Rooney appeared in the doorway.

Midge crept toward the snake.

Officer Rooney, a petite woman in her thirties, bravely touched the back of Gunther's long, scaly body with the toe of her boot.

Gunther swung his head away from Faith and Watson.

While the snake was distracted, Midge seized Gunther right behind his head. She put Gunther back into the cooler and secured the lid, then breathed a sigh of relief that mirrored Faith's own.

"Watson squirmed out of my arms and ran off before I could catch him," Midge explained, joining Faith and scratching the cat's chin. "I knew he would protect you. My money wasn't on Gunther in that confrontation."

Chief Garris regarded Faith. "Are you all right?"

Faith nodded. There was an enormous lump in her throat, and she still felt too shaken to speak. She clutched Watson closer to her chest.

Garris seemed to understand her discomfort. "We can go upstairs now," he suggested gently, placing a strong hand under her elbow.

Faith let the chief help her out of the tunnel as quickly as her quaking legs would allow.

If I never come back down here, it'll be too soon.

21

Sunlight streamed through the windows and cascaded over them as they emerged from the top of the staircase. Faith had never been so happy to be aboveground in her life. She cuddled Watson close and told herself she was completely safe.

Until she remembered that she didn't know what had happened to Philip.

"Philip Peters is responsible for taking Gunther out of his enclosure and hiding him," Faith said. "Maybe it's not too late to stop him from leaving the property."

"We got here just in time to intercept him. I think he was trying to leave without a proper checkout," the chief said with a smile.

"How did you know it was him?" Faith asked.

"Midge told us someone had stashed Ms. Perkins's snake in the tunnels," Garris explained. "So when we met Midge at the front door and saw Mr. Peters in a hurry to leave, we stopped him. It doesn't take years of experience in law enforcement to know the guy trying to flee the scene is often the one you want."

Midge and Officer Rooney caught up with them, hauling the cooler between them.

Faith studied Midge. "Are you okay?"

"Oh, this is all in a day's work for me," Midge said. "That's one of the best parts about my job. I never know what to expect. His terrarium is in the conservatory, right?"

"Yes," Faith said. She watched with relief as Midge and the officer took the snake away.

"I have some news I think you'll want to hear," the chief said. "We found the murder weapon in Judge Davidson's suite."

"Are you sure?" Faith asked.

"The autopsy results showed tiny fibers on Ms. Marsden's neck. A dresser scarf in the room had matching fibers. The judge's fingerprints were all over the dresser, and we also found matching fibers under his nails."

"So you're certain he killed her?" Faith said.

Garris nodded. "Between the fibers and the note Ms. Marsden left, the evidence is solid. We believe the judge murdered Ms. Marsden because he thought she knew more about his crimes than she really did. Or he didn't want to take the chance that she'd go to the police and get an investigation started."

"So who killed the judge?" Faith asked. "Was it Philip? If so, did he give you an explanation?" He'd seemed guilty, but then again, he hadn't actually confessed.

"So far, Mr. Peters has refused to speak at all," the chief said.

"I would have had some evidence," Faith said bitterly, "but he broke the cell phone I was using to record him."

"You mean this?" Garris held up the phone, its screen cracked into a sunburst pattern. "I thought it might be important. Otherwise, why would someone try to destroy it?" He handed Faith the phone.

Faith ran her thumb gently over the broken surface. To her surprise, it came to life. "This thing is tougher than it looks, but let's see if my video is still there." Careful not to damage the screen any further, she tapped again, and the video began to play.

"Why don't you come with me?" he asked. "We'll show Mr. Peters your recording together. I'll be happy for anything that will help loosen his lips. And then we'll give your phone to the techs so they can get everything off it before it dies completely."

Unsure she was ready to face her would-be murderer, Faith looked down at Watson.

The cat blinked at her slowly.

She smiled, gave him a final squeeze, then placed him gently on the floor. "If you think it will help get to the bottom of what happened to the judge, then I'd be happy to."

"I hoped you'd say that, and I'll be right there the whole time," the chief said. "I expect it would take more than a run-in with a bad guy and a giant snake to sideline you."

Faith felt the glow that came with a sincere compliment flooding through her body. She did not always think of herself as a particularly brave person, but she did like to lend a hand and do the right thing. She realized that sometimes it required bravery, and she was grateful that when it did, she was not found wanting.

Garris led Faith to a staff room in the basement, where he had set up a command center for the investigation.

Watson followed, obviously still considering himself on duty.

Philip slumped in a chair with Officer Bryan Laddy towering over him. Philip glanced at Faith as she entered the room.

She thought she saw a flicker of remorse pass over his face. Faith wasn't sure if it was on account of the harm he had tried to cause her or the fact that she was safe and able to tell her story.

Faith took a seat across from Philip. Despite the warmth of the day, she felt a shiver run along her shoulders as she regarded the man, who had seemed so good and had done so much bad.

Garris sat down next to Faith. "May I have your phone?"

Faith handed it to him with a sense of relief. It was out of her hands now.

As the chief played the recording, Faith kept her gaze firmly fixed on Philip. She had no desire to revisit the terror she had felt in the tunnels by watching the scene. Just hearing the audio that accompanied the images was harrowing enough.

Philip seemed stricken too.

She wondered why. He'd already confessed to letting the snake loose in order to frighten the judge into having a fatal heart attack, and he'd probably murdered him. Or was he upset because he'd been caught?

When the video ended, Garris turned off Faith's cell phone and placed it out of Philip's reach on the table.

Philip sighed deeply, then leaned forward in his chair.

Faith felt her whole body tense.

Watson must have noticed her reaction because he sprang from the floor into her lap and faced Philip with his ears flattened against his head. Faith heard him growl.

"That's quite the little tiger you've got there," Philip said with the ghost of a smile playing on his lips. "I have to admire him despite everything. I wouldn't have expected a small cat to hold off a huge python."

"I can understand you wanting to get back at the judge for awarding you so little in your lawsuit," the chief said. "But trying to frighten him to death seems extreme."

"It had nothing to do with the lawsuit," Philip said, shaking his head.

"Why did you do it, then?" Faith asked.

Philip stared down at the floor as if the answer to her question could be found in the plush carpeting at his feet. Finally, he lifted his gaze and tightened his jaw as if he'd reached a decision. "It was his memoir."

Garris pulled his ever-present notepad and pen from his pocket and started scribbling on a blank sheet of paper. "Was he about to share something in it that you didn't want to become public? Was he blackmailing you?"

Blackmail. The thought had never occurred to Faith, though it would explain a few things.

"No, it was not a case of blackmail," Philip replied. He paused before adding, "Although I suppose I could have blackmailed the judge if I'd been able to unearth the evidence."

"If it wasn't blackmail, then what was it?" Faith asked.

"It did involve the story he was going to tell," Philip admitted. "But it wasn't a matter of exposing a secret. Well, not entirely."

"Stop talking in riddles," the chief said. "What were you trying to do?"

"I didn't want the judge to profit from someone else's tragedy," Philip answered.

"Whose tragedy?" Garris pressed.

Philip sighed. "This is all going to come out, and I'm probably a dead man anyway, so I might as well tell you. Philip Peters is not my real name. It was one I chose after I was placed in the witness protection program."

Faith didn't know what she'd been expecting, but this certainly wasn't it.

"Can you tell me why you were placed in the program?" the chief asked, glancing over at Officer Laddy.

"I'm not sure that it even matters now," Philip said. "It was because of the St. James case."

"I remember that case," Garris said, looking thoughtful. "It was big news at the time."

"Yes, and there has been occasional renewed interest about it over the years," Philip said.

"Two parents were killed, and their young son was left injured," the chief continued.

Philip nodded, and Faith thought she saw tears in his eyes. "The little boy was me." His voice broke.

"It was an organized crime case," Garris said. "I seem to remember that your father had planned to testify about some financial ties a mob family had to a number of prominent local politicians."

"That's right," Philip said. "My father worked as an accountant, and he uncovered a trail of dirty money. He was brave and honest, and he wanted to help the police. He couldn't stand by and do nothing."

"Judge Davidson presided over the case," the chief stated. "It was quite a controversial ruling, wasn't it?"

"You could say that," Philip said bitterly. "There were rumors that the judge had been bribed to allow the defendant off on a technicality."

"Do you believe them?" Faith asked, horrified.

"I had always suspected that the judge did not act impartially," Philip answered. "When I ended up in front of him myself with the lawsuit against Terrence Hoyle, I was sure of it."

"How did you know that the judge was going to write his memoir?" Garris asked.

"My wife, Janine, has been to several workshops for writing memoirs, and she met the judge at one of them," Philip responded. "There was no way I was going to allow the judge to benefit from my parents' murders. Especially after they didn't receive justice in his courtroom."

A new thought occurred to Faith. "It was your idea for Janine to recommend the manor for a writers retreat."

"Yes," Philip said. "After one of her workshops, Janine brought home an evaluation form to fill out, and she showed it to me. I suggested Castleton would be a perfect place for a writers retreat because of the Laura Ingalls Wilder theme and the log cabin project."

"Did your wife have any idea why you wanted to come here this week?" the chief said. "Was she part of your plan to do away with Judge Davidson?"

Faith thought back to Janine's quest for a hot-water bottle. Had she known that her husband wanted it for Gunther rather than himself? Had that sweet, enthusiastic woman been as determined to stop the judge from writing his memoirs as her husband? Had she tried to frame Cody for the murder?

"She had no idea what I was up to," Philip said. "She doesn't even know that I'm living under a false name."

"She doesn't know you're in the witness protection program?" Faith was shocked. She couldn't imagine failing to share such an important part of her life with someone she chose to marry. But she also couldn't imagine going through with a plan to harm another person.

"That's part of the witness protection program," Philip snapped.

"You don't go around telling people you're in it. Besides, it's a painful part of my past that I would rather not dredge up."

"So Janine really thought the hot-water bottle was for you?" Faith asked.

Philip nodded. "I told her my allergies were bothering me and I needed one."

"Why a hot-water bottle?" the chief asked.

"I wanted to use a heating pad or a lamp for the snake, but I couldn't find any electrical outlets in the tunnels."

"But my cat found a hot-water bottle in Cody's duffel bag," Faith said.

"I didn't expect Janine to ask the staff for one," Philip said. "When I found out, I bought a bottle in town and planted it in Cody's bag with his juggling supplies. Then I told Janine that I suspected he'd taken it from our room." He shrugged. "It was the best I could do."

"This was a carefully orchestrated plan that seemed to depend on a lot of variables out of your control," Garris said. "How did you manage it?"

"It wasn't as difficult as you might think," Philip said. "Janine took my interest in the workshop as enthusiasm for her project. It was easy to work subtle questions about the other attendees into the conversation."

"How did you know who would be attending the retreat?" Faith asked.

"I told Janine she should offer to set up an online group for the attendees to interact and get to know each other before the retreat," Philip said. "Pamela thought it was a great idea, and she gave Janine the list of names."

"And the judge was on it?" Faith asked.

"Of course he was," Philip answered. "According to Janine, he was adamant about writing his memoirs."

"It must have worried you when he had to have surgery," Faith said.

"Was that the surgery Ms. Marsden mentioned in the note she left?" the chief asked.

"That's the one," Faith said.

"I hadn't expected it," Philip admitted. "But I figured he might die on the operating table, which would have kept me clean and been an even easier way to keep him from publishing his memoir."

Faith felt repulsed by his callous words. He must have been carrying some very deep wounds to have so little regard for another human life.

"The judge recovered in time for the retreat after all," Garris said. "We've gotten the autopsy report back, and it turns out that the judge was strangled by a ligature rather than a python. I assume that you were responsible for that."

"It felt like fate was playing right into my hands," Philip said, seeming to almost warm to his story. "Janine told me that during the workshop where she met the judge, the writers had talked about their personal phobias, and the judge admitted that he was frightened to death of snakes. I realized I had the opportunity I had been waiting for."

"What did you do exactly?" the chief asked, scribbling in his notepad.

"I took Gunther from the conservatory almost as soon as Fiona arrived with him," Philip replied. "I knew that she would be likely to travel with her pet snake since she's famous for taking it with her wherever she goes."

"Did you plan to blame the crime on Gunther?" Faith asked.

"Not at first," Philip answered. "Like I told you in the tunnel, I hoped the judge's heart condition was delicate enough that the mere idea of a snake on the loose in the manor would be enough to bring on a heart attack."

"But it didn't work out that easily, did it?" Faith asked.

"No. When the nurse died, I hoped he would be in an even more fragile state, but he was tougher and luckier than I had imagined."

Faith had another disturbing thought. "Did you set the fire at the log cabin? Did you hope to kill him that way?"

"That was quite clever of me, wasn't it?" Philip said, an unpleasant gleam in his eye.

"How did you do it?" Faith persisted. "You weren't near the log cabin when the fire broke out."

"Earlier in the day, I placed a remote fire-starting device on the back of the cabin," Philip said. "It was a simple enough thing to wait until the judge was inside and then to head up to meet the rest of you. At the push of a button, I was able to start the fire from a distance."

"And while we were all occupied with the judge and tossing buckets of water on the building, you sneaked around back and removed the device." Faith shook her head. The plan was so simple that it was ingenious. Although it hadn't quite worked.

"I pried it off the building and slipped it into my pocket before coming around front with the rest of you," Philip said. "But my timing was off. If I'd been able to stall you all a little longer before we got to the cabin, the judge might have died of smoke inhalation. As it was, I had to help you rescue him to keep my cover."

"In the end, you did manage to kill him," the chief accused.

Philip nodded. "It was remarkably easy when I took matters into my own hands and stopped trying to keep the deed at arm's length."

"Tell me how you did it," Garris said.

"I got him on his own one day and told him that I wanted to let bygones be bygones," Philip said.

"Bygones about your parents' case or bygones about your own lawsuit against Terrence Hoyle?" the chief said.

"The case against Terrence," Philip answered. "The judge didn't know who I really was. He never recognized me as the bereft child who had been in his courtroom so many years earlier."

"How does your fake olive branch turn into luring the judge into the covered wagon?" Faith asked.

"I offered to give him a private tour of the log cabin from the architect's perspective," Philip said. "I told him we should visit the cabin before everyone showed up for dinner."

"Did you throw in the covered wagon as part of the tour?" Faith asked.

"He didn't care that it wasn't mine to offer," Philip said. "He was only too happy to scramble up in there. I climbed in after him and looped the scarf I'd brought with me around his neck."

Faith could not help but acknowledge the cleverness of the plan. Philip had adapted to the circumstances and made them work to support his own goals.

Perhaps his thoroughness was a quality that any architect must possess. Faith was not sure anyone would ever know. Certainly, his early loss of his parents and his perceived lack of justice for their deaths would have made his worldview unlike that of most other men.

"Did you hope at the time that Fiona's snake would be blamed for his death?" Faith said.

"The thought had crossed my mind," Philip said. "That's why it shows such a wide ligature. It seemed about the same width as that snake. And it was meant to look like the same manner of death that the nurse suffered, so whoever—or whatever—was blamed for her death would also get the blame for the judge's. It should have been a neat, tidy little package, with Cody taking the fall for everything." He shook his head, as if he couldn't quite believe he'd been caught.

"I think that about covers everything," the chief said. "Do you have any other questions, Faith?"

She had a great number of unanswered questions, but most of them were moral in nature. There remained only three questions on her mind about the actual case.

"I thought someone was eavesdropping on Diana and me when we were out walking together shortly before she died," Faith told Philip. "Was it you?"

"I was taking a walk, and I wondered how much Diana knew about her boss. I thought she might let something slip to you if she did."

"Why would you think she would tell me anything?" Faith asked.

"You have the sort of character that invites confidences," Philip said. "Even my own wife commented on it to me."

Faith wasn't sure how she felt about that, so she went on. "Speaking of Janine, she mentioned that the timing for this retreat was perfect because you were having smoke damage cleaned at your home. Did you set that fire too?"

Garris glanced at Faith. He probably hadn't heard about the fire at the Peters' home. She hadn't had a chance to tell him, and she didn't think anyone else who knew would have thought to inform him.

"We were completely broke," Philip said. "The lawsuit against Terrence Hoyle wasn't a frivolous one. I needed the settlement. When the judge awarded me only one dollar in that lawsuit, even though Hoyle had bankrupted me, I had to come up with a way to raise some cash."

"So you decided to set the fire in order to collect the insurance money?" the chief asked.

"I set up a delayed timer that was similar to the one I used at the log cabin in order to have an alibi for the time of the fire," Philip said. "I thought I was going to get away with it too, but then someone got nosy." He glared at Faith.

Faith avoided his gaze and stared down at Watson cuddled up and purring in her lap. How could he seem so fresh and content when she felt so drained? The flood of adrenaline had left her body, and she felt weak and wrung out as her body pressed against the chair beneath her.

"Were you really hoping that the snake would kill me?" she asked in a low voice, not sure she wanted the answer.

"Let's put it this way," Philip said. "I wasn't planning for you to make it out of there alive."

Garris stood. "Fortunately, your plans don't seem to work very well. It's high time we took you to the station."

22

Faith slept in the next morning with Watson curled up on the quilt beside her.

She had talked to Wolfe for a long time last night. Even though he'd made her feel better, she had awakened several times during the night, haunted by dreams of snakes and fires and being trapped in dark places underground. Each time she opened her eyes, Watson snuggled closer to her and pressed his head against her body, purring loudly. She was grateful for his warm, comforting presence.

Ordinarily she would have felt guilty about oversleeping, but she didn't this morning. The disturbing events of the last few days had taken their toll, and she needed some extra sleep. Besides, she wasn't expected to open the library until later than usual, so there was no need to rush.

Eventually, she slid out of her cozy bed and prepared to meet her day. Faith took her time in the shower and then lingered over her breakfast. She gave Watson an extra couple of tunaroons. After all, he'd probably saved her life the day before.

It was the final day of the memoir writers retreat. The number of visitors was sadly diminished after two deaths and one arrest.

Despite Philip's attempt on her life, she still felt sorry for the bereaved child who had turned into such a damaged man. She could not quite believe that someone who had brought such artistry and care to the creation of the log cabin could also be so bent on destructiveness and revenge.

Watson trotted along at her side as she made her way from the cottage to the manor, and she was more grateful for his companionship than usual.

Faith looked forward to the last session of the retreat. Pamela's small group of writers planned to give a final reading of their works in progress. The event was originally scheduled to be held inside the log cabin, but Pamela had asked Faith if they could use the library instead. Faith had readily agreed to host the session. She knew how painful it would be for the group to return to the cabin—the scene of so many unpleasant memories.

No matter what Philip and the judge had done, Faith could not help but feel fondness toward the little log cabin, the covered wagon, and of course the happy memories she associated with the works of Laura Ingalls Wilder.

When they entered the manor, Watson took off down the hall.

Faith watched his bobbed tail disappear with a faint sense of regret before she continued to the library. She unlocked the door and paused in front of the alcove where she had placed the collection of Wilder's works and those written about her and her world by others. She picked up *By the Shores of Silver Lake* at random and took a moment to read a few pages.

Pamela had been wise to encourage her students to take note of the expert way Wilder had brought her stories to life. Wilder had simply but brilliantly portrayed a testament to the resilience of loving families. As Faith slid the book back onto the shelf, she felt the familiar peace she always did when rereading one of her favorite books. It was like visiting an old friend.

Faith checked the room to be sure everything was set for the reading. She moved a few more chairs to the cozy grouping placed before the enormous fireplace. Then she fetched the tall dictionary stand to serve as a makeshift podium.

Just before the guests arrived, Faith remembered to call down to the kitchen to double-check that Brooke knew that refreshments no longer needed to be sent to the cabin.

Faith greeted Pamela and the others as they filed into the library, then pointed them to the chairs in front of the fireplace.

Marlene entered the room and strode over to Faith. "It seems as if everything's in order," she said, glancing around.

Faith nodded. "I made sure Brooke is aware of the change of location too."

"Good." Marlene went to mingle with some of the guests.

A moment later, Pamela approached the podium. "Welcome to the final session of our writers retreat. I want to thank all of you for attending. It's been a difficult time, but we've managed to get through it. Maybe it'll even make it into some of your pieces. Now, who would like to start?"

Each of the writers took a turn at the podium. In no time, Faith found herself caught up in their stories.

She was surprised to see that Marlene had taken a break from her professional duties to stay and listen to their readings as well. Faith thought the assistant manager seemed to be enjoying herself.

She was even more surprised that Janine was one of the readers. Faith had expected her to be too consumed with worry over her husband to make time for such an activity. She appeared decidedly less perky than usual, but she bravely rose to the occasion and read from her own work.

At the conclusion of the readings, Faith and Marlene escorted the guests to the salon, where the refreshments table was set up for all the small groups to enjoy.

Faith approached Brooke, who was overseeing the food.

"I heard what happened yesterday with the snake and Philip," Brooke whispered. "I can't believe it."

"I can't either," Faith admitted. "I wanted to tell you—"

Before she could say anything else, Marlene bustled over and studied the table. "Is there enough coffee?"

"I'll get some more," Brooke said, apparently catching the hint, though there was plenty of coffee. She gave Faith an apologetic smile and hurried away.

Faith would have to catch up with Brooke later. She turned to the guests and decided to speak to each of the writers. First, she approached Fiona, who stood next to Cody.

Fiona was dressed as flamboyantly as usual in a bead-encrusted magenta dress. It could have been taken straight out of a photograph from the roaring twenties.

Faith was surprised to see that Athena sat dutifully at the magician's side, her leash in Fiona's gloved hand. She also noticed with relief that the python was nowhere in sight. Instead, Fiona wore a long feather boa draped over her shoulders.

"Where's Gunther?" Faith asked.

"I thought everyone might feel better if I left him securely in his terrarium, which has been moved to my suite and is under lock and key," Fiona said, fingering her feather boa. "It seems extreme, but I really didn't want to worry about another disappearing act from him."

"I added another latch and weighted the top of the screen down with a few additional cinder blocks that I borrowed from the maintenance staff just to be sure," Cody chimed in.

"But you're not without animal companionship, I see," Faith said. She bent down and held out her hand for Athena to sniff.

The little dog made a grunting noise, then turned away as if to refuse the overture of friendship.

Faith decided it must be because of Athena's dislike for Watson. There was simply no accounting for taste.

"It's hardly her fault that her master went and got himself killed," Fiona said. "Someone had to give the sweet baby a good home, and it might as well be me."

"That's very kind of you," Faith said.

"I thought it would be fun to have something warm-blooded other than Cody around for a change," Fiona said. "Besides, I can picture her decked out with a rhinestone collar and leash and a tiny purple cape. I can tell she's got a natural flair, and that old man was suppressing it.

Animals have as much right to be themselves as humans do, you know."

Faith smiled. She imagined that Fiona and Athena would get along quite well. It seemed that both of them had unusual taste.

"I enjoyed your reading a great deal," Faith said. "You had quite a remarkable story to tell. I can't wait for it to be published so I can read it in its entirety."

"Thank you," Fiona said. "I'm happy to know that you enjoyed it."

Faith thought she heard a smile in the woman's tone, though she couldn't be sure because of the heavy black netting of the magician's veil.

"But I have decided not to seek publication for my book."

"You've changed your mind?" Faith asked, surprised.

"The past few days have opened my eyes to the evil that comes from harboring resentments," Fiona said. "I'd hoped that writing my memoir would be cathartic, but it has only served to stoke my anger about the injustice of my court case. I don't wish to spend the rest of my life feeling miserable and wallowing in the past. I've been doing that a lot, even physically shrouding myself in a reminder of it."

Faith didn't know what to say.

Fiona reached up a gloved hand and gripped her veil. "I think it's time to let go of this too." With a flourish, she pulled the veil off.

Underneath was the face of a woman in her late fifties or early sixties. She had a shock of short white hair, piercing hazel eyes, and a well-defined nose and chin. A faint scar ran up one side of her neck and onto her cheek, but Faith wouldn't have noticed it if she hadn't been looking for some sign of the accident that had marked the magician years before.

"Fiona," Faith murmured, "you're lovely."

Color suffused her cheeks. "My scar isn't hideous?"

"Not at all," Faith assured her. "It simply adds a rakish element to your appearance."

Fiona beamed at her. "That I can live with."

Faith had to admire the woman's change of heart. It was not easy to let go of past hurts and hostilities. "Do you have any idea what you'll do now instead of writing your memoir and hiding behind a veil?"

Fiona nodded. "I've decided that rather than have my story live on in a dusty old book that likely few people will read, it would be a far better legacy to share everything I know with my apprentice. Not only the common tricks. We're going to make him a star."

Cody, who had clearly been as thunderstruck as Faith by his boss's unveiling, now gave a smile that said his dreams had come true.

Faith smiled. "That's wonderful news. Congratulations, Cody. You must be thrilled to be learning from such an expert."

"I couldn't have asked for a happier ending to my own story," Cody said. With a polite bow, he swept his hat from his head, then offered Fiona his arm.

They swooped out of the room, with Athena trotting along at their side.

As Faith was turning back toward the group, she felt gentle pressure on her elbow. She turned to see Christina and Terrence standing at her side.

"We wanted to be sure to say goodbye to you before we checked out," Christina said.

"I'm glad you did," Faith said.

Prunella's little head poked out of Christina's designer handbag, her nose twitching in the air.

Christina smiled at the small creature. "Thank you again for helping to return her to me."

"It was my pleasure," Faith said. "I'm sorry this week wasn't exactly what we'd hoped or planned."

"The whole experience has been stressful," Terrence said. "In fact, we're taking a vacation to recover from our vacation."

"I can't wait." Christina gazed adoringly at her husband and leaned her head against his shoulder.

"Where are you going?" Faith asked.

"A beachfront resort in the Caribbean," Christina replied. "We're going to fly down there tomorrow morning and stay for a couple of weeks."

"That sounds lovely," Faith said. "I hope you have a wonderful time."

"The best part of it is the whole vacation will be tax deductible," Terrence said. "I plan to check out some properties for potential development while we're there."

"Isn't he clever?" Christina smiled. "And such a talented writer too."

Faith agreed. She had found Terrence's reading particularly engaging. "I hope that you'll feel encouraged to continue writing, even though the retreat wasn't exactly smooth. I think your manuscript showed a lot of promise."

"I appreciate your saying that," Terrence said. "I do intend to continue writing. Being here this week has given me even more to include in my memoir."

"You plan to include the murders in your book?" Faith asked, startled.

"I'd be a fool not to," Terrence said, flashing her a giant smile. "After all, people love mysteries."

"We'd better be on our way," Christina said. "I need time to pack for our trip if we're going to leave tomorrow morning."

Faith watched as they walked to the door. It was ironic that Philip had murdered the judge to keep him from writing about his parents' deaths when the cause of the judge's murder sounded likely to end up in Terrence's own memoir.

Janine stood at the refreshments table, staring at the food but clearly not seeing it.

Faith went over and placed a hand gently on her shoulder. "Thank you for coming to the reading this morning."

"I wasn't sure if I would be welcome," Janine admitted softly. "But Pamela said that Philip's actions had nothing to do with me and that it would be a shame for me to miss out."

"Pamela was right," Faith said. "Even though Philip is your husband, you're not responsible for what he did. He told the police that you didn't even know about his past."

"I didn't. I knew he was an orphan, but he never liked to talk about his childhood. Now I wonder whether he ever told me the truth about anything."

Faith could not imagine how devastating it had been for Janine to learn that her husband was a murderer and the life they had built together meant less to him than a need for revenge. The poor woman had had her whole world flipped upside down in a matter of hours.

"I always knew that something was troubling him," Janine said. "But I assumed it was just problems with our marriage caused by our differing schedules. I didn't realize it was far more than that. He hid that part of himself very well. The man I married was a completely different person than I thought he was."

Philip had certainly been a great actor to conceal so much of himself from his wife. "Do you have somewhere to stay?" Faith asked.

"I'm going to move in with my sister," Janine said. "I plan to set aside my writing and devote all my energy to helping others."

"What will you be doing?"

"I want to counsel children dealing with tragedies," Janine replied. "If Philip had had help when his parents were killed, then maybe he wouldn't have done the things he did. I want to do everything I can to make sure other people don't go through something like this."

"That's an admirable goal," Faith said. "Are you planning to earn a degree in counseling?"

Janine nodded. "And I plan to do some volunteer work while I take classes."

As she spoke, Faith couldn't help but notice that her face brightened, as if simply discussing improving others' lives brought back some of her trademark vitality. Faith got the impression that even finding out her husband was a murderer wouldn't keep Janine down for long.

When Janine left, Faith noticed Pamela sitting by herself. The writers group leader turned and gave Faith a tired smile as she approached.

"I have truly enjoyed meeting you," Faith told her. "I hope what happened during the retreat doesn't leave you with any bad memories of the manor."

"I have nothing but admiration for this estate and its wonderful staff," Pamela assured her. "Though I have had my fill of writers."

"I'm sorry to hear that," Faith said. "It's hard when other people complicate a job you enjoy."

"Actually I've been considering a career change for some time, and this retreat helped to make a tough decision a whole lot easier."

"What will you do instead?"

"I've been offered a job as an interpreter at a living history museum," Pamela said, a spark of excitement in her eyes.

"Is it one of those museums where the staff act as though they are living in the time period that the museum represents?"

Pamela nodded. "It's a museum devoted to the American pioneer era. In truth, it's exactly what I've always wanted to do, ever since I first read the Laura Ingalls Wilder books."

"Congratulations. Will you be taking your covered wagon with you, or does it hold too many bad memories?"

"Well, I wouldn't be much good as a pioneer if I let a natural occurrence like a death dissuade me from continuing to drive my covered wagon farther west," Pamela said. "In a small way, I feel as though the difficulties have prepared me more thoroughly for the interpreter job."

"I'm so glad that things have worked out for you," Faith said, marveling at Pamela's outstanding attitude after everything that had gone wrong. The woman was every bit as hardy as Laura Ingalls Wilder.

"Thank you. I can't wait to get started. They've asked me to begin my duties by driving the covered wagon to the museum. I'll be taking the same route the pioneers traveled and documenting the journey on my blog. My favorite part is that I'll follow the same path the Ingalls family took once I reach Wisconsin."

"What a fascinating idea," Faith remarked. It was clear to see that Pamela's enthusiasm for the project was almost bubbling over. "I'll be sure to keep up with your blog."

"I appreciate it, and I hope you'll share it with your friends. I need to go and tend to Stormy. He has a long trip ahead of him." Pamela grinned and waved. "Thanks for everything."

Faith sat on the loggia at the manor, enjoying the lovely weather with Eileen, Brooke, Midge, Wolfe, and Marlene. The writers retreat was officially over, Wolfe was back from his business trip, and they all had a lot to catch up on.

Brooke had graciously contributed tea and coffee and a plate of scones, muffins, and cinnamon rolls to their impromptu get-together. The others eagerly helped themselves to the delicious goodies.

Watson was sitting on Faith's lap, eyeing the blueberry scone on her plate.

"It's hard to believe that so much happened while I was gone," Wolfe remarked.

"There never seems to be a dull moment around here," Marlene said, her tone dry.

"Such a tragic week," Eileen murmured. "Two deaths, two missing pets, and a fire at the brand-new log cabin."

"Who would have thought that the judge and Philip were murderers?" Brooke asked.

"Or that Philip would try to frame Cody for everything?" Faith added.

"Revenge and bitterness certainly have a way of ruining people's lives," Midge said as she poured herself a cup of coffee. "We've seen ample evidence of that lately."

"That's why I was so glad to hear that Fiona is going to give up her memoir and her veil," Faith said. "She's letting go of the past."

"That's amazing news," Brooke responded, pinching off a bite of her cinnamon roll.

"What will she do instead?" Eileen asked.

"She's going to teach Cody everything she knows about magic." Faith smiled. "And she has a new sidekick. The judge's bulldog, Athena."

"I wonder how Gunther will feel about that," Eileen said. "By the way, I still can't believe that you and Midge faced down a ten-foot python."

Watson meowed as if to say, "What about me?"

"You too, Rumpy," Faith said as she scratched behind his ears. "You were the most heroic of all when you stood up to Gunther to protect me."

"It was definitely one of the more unusual animal encounters I've ever had," Midge admitted.

"That sounds like an understatement," Wolfe said.

"One thing still puzzles me," Eileen said. "How did all these people end up in the same writers group?"

"I was wondering the same thing," Faith answered, "so I asked Pamela right before she left. She said they all joined her small group after attending her workshop in Boston."

"Has anyone seen my phone?" Marlene suddenly asked, scanning the table.

Brooke, who was sitting next to Marlene, snatched it up from the space between them. "If it was a snake, it would have bitten you."

Everyone broke into laughter.

Faith smiled at the warm, cheerful faces surrounding her. Even though it had been a difficult week, she felt nothing but gratitude for her friends, her job, and the support of the caring man beside her who had not let go of her hand since he'd sat down.

When she'd heard about Pamela's upcoming journey, Faith had felt a pang of envy, but the feeling was fleeting. As she gazed around the loggia now, Faith knew that she was exactly where she wanted to be.

Castleton Manor had a way of providing more than enough adventure for her.

YOUR FEEDBACK MEANS A LOT TO US!

Up to this point, we've been doing all the writing. Now it's *your* turn!

Tell us what you think about this book, the characters, the bad guy, or anything else you'd like to share with us about this series. We can't wait to hear from *you!*

Log on to give us your feedback at:
https://www.surveymonkey.com/r/CastletonLibrary

Annie's® FICTION